KINTSUGI

Celebrating
30 Years of Publishing
in India

PRAISE FOR KINTSUGI

'I was mesmerized by the quiet beauty of this novel. With a tender yet unflinching gaze, Anukrti Upadhyay tells us the stories of extraordinary young women who craft for themselves the lives that they desire, memorable characters who are shaped, but never defined, by their grief and heartbreak. *Kintsugi* is about many things – devotion, loyalty, ambition, and desire – but most of all, it is a novel about resilience and courage.'

– AMRITA MAHALE, author of *Milk Teeth*

'I loved *Kintsugi* ... How the characters' connections/ conjunctions never felt forced, kept surprising me; how the sentences weren't overwritten or straining for poetry, but also never bland or banal.'

– DEBORAH SMITH, translator of *The Vegetarian* by Han Kang

'The finest novel I read in 2020 ... It gladdened my heart.'

– KEKI DARUWALLA

'Delightful ... there's a certain quality to her writing that is both deep and light, very like the artistry of the jewellers that are the heart of this piece of writing.'

– OMAIR AHMAD

'*Kintsugi* is a delicate work about the many ways the heart remakes itself, that like an ornament slowly being chiselled and laid takes time to reveal its final shape. Yet by its end ... its artistry is evident, and despite its title, seamlessly expressed.'

– SHARANYA MANIVANNAN, author of *The High Priestess Never Marries*

'What a book! Mesmerizing ... delicate and deep.'

– SHOBHAA DE

'Each character's individual presence is like a piece of life that comes together, melded gracefully by Upadhyay's writing. Her prose, spare and simple, takes shape delicately...'

– *Asian Review of Books*

'A little gem ... Upadhyay's writing has restraint, poise and an understated charm, with no room for superfluity.'

– *Hindustan Times*

'A rich, character-driven story that flows more or less linearly, and with a quiet beauty of language that seeks to work in aid of telling the story without drawing attention to itself. Read it for a little healing in these anxious times.'

– *Mint*

'In *Kintsugi*, the author shows the extraordinary strength inherent in the lives of ordinary people if only they had the courage to tap into it without fear ... A novel that echoes with loneliness, loss, longing, and unfulfilled promises.'

– *Open*

'The stories exist in a quiet zone ... there is more unsaid than said ... yet we are drawn into the lives of these six people almost immediately. And we are shown again and again, just how the human heart and its longings remain the same from person to person ... Easily one of the best books [of] 2020.'

– *The New Indian Express*

'A beautifully crafted novel based on the central idea of "kintsugi" or the skill of joining fragmented bits with precious artistry, the quiet flow of emotions is richly nuanced. While the novel reads easily due to an engrossing plot line, the complex narrative is woven with finesse to leave no loose ends. The author builds a web of life that is authentic to the cultures but transcends them to reach towards a universal humanism. A remarkable feat in imaginative extension and also firmly grounded on cultural reality, this book holds a wide appeal for a global literary audience.'

– THE SUSHILA DEVI AWARD 2021 JURY

KINTSUGI

A Novel

Anukrti Upadhyay

FOURTH ESTATE · *New Delhi*

First published in hardback in India by Fourth Estate 2020
An imprint of HarperCollins *Publishers*
4th Floor, Tower A, Building No. 10, Phase II, DLF Cyber City,
Gurugram, Haryana – 122002
www.harpercollins.co.in

This edition published in India 2023

2 4 6 8 10 9 7 5 3 1

P-ISBN: 978-93-5629-298-7
E-ISBN: 978-93-5357-954-8

The title of this book uses typefaces created by hand in collaboration with craftswomen from Karnataka (Radha Sullur | Chittara); Kutch (Rathore Paani ben, Hetal ben, Chare Lata ben, Amisha ben, Manisha ben, Varsha ben, Ramila ben and Gita ben | Soof embroidery); Barmer, Rajasthan (Chunni, Shanti, Tibu, Pawani, Paami, Bhaami, Mangi, Khetu, Anita, Nirmala, Shanti, Jasoda, Chandi and Kastura Ram | Barmer applique) and from Chhattisgarh (Ram Keli Pavle, Sunita Pavle, Sumitra Pavle | Gond tribal tattoos). These were made as part of the Typecraft Initiative (www.typecraftinitiative.org) to support, innovate and promote Indian crafts and culture through design and the digital medium.

Typeset in 10.5/15 Scala at
Manipal Technologies Limited, Manipal

Printed and bound at
Thomson Press (India) Ltd

A pebble drops
Waves touch
Unseen shores...

HARUKO

HARUKO CROUCHED BEFORE a small clay furnace. The furnace was old, the plaster-and-clay chamber under the curved clay tile was filled with the ashes of innumerable firings. She placed the carefully weighed lumps of gold and silver into a crusty, blackened, old clay bowl and slid it into the furnace. She settled back on her heels and flicked the switch on the blowtorch. The hissing drone of the gas-powered torch filled the room as she sent the blue flame flickering into the womb of the furnace, passing and re-passing it over the pieces of metal nestled in the bowl.

'That's enough!' Madanji called out over the trembling sound, even as Haruko switched the torch off. She knew all about the melting points of different materials from her courses in metalwork at the design school. In the six months she had been at Madanji's gaddi, she had melted metals several times each day. Taking an old pair of iron tongs thickly coated with ashes, she drew the clay bowl out and examined the flame-darkened metals. They were fused together into a sluggish, semi-liquid mass. She set the bowl aside to allow the alloy to cool. Later, she would pull it into sheets or wires as needed on the large lathe which occupied a quarter of the gaddi.

The gaddi where Haruko worked was a set of low-ceilinged rooms in a large three-storeyed haveli built by Madanji's great-grandfather. The rooms had wooden desks ranged along the walls on three sides, each with a cotton-filled floor seat spread over the thick mattress covering the floor. It was this floor seat of the jewellers and artisans – the gaddi – from which jewellery shops derived their generic name, Madanji had explained to her on her first day. The haveli stood in a narrow street, one among a network of similar streets radiating from the main jewellers' market, the famous Johri Bazaar. Besides housing the ancestral gaddi, the haveli was also Madanji's family home. Haruko had been living here too since she had arrived in Jaipur, in a tiny windowless room on the third floor, up steep flights of high, stone steps. The thick-walled room was always cool and opened on to a wide terrace. In the evenings, after the work at the gaddi was over, Haruko spent her time on the terrace, drawing or reading under her solar lamp. All around, as far as she could see, were old havelis, pink and white, slim and tall, stranded like ships.

Besides Madanji, a plump, fair-complexioned man of fifty or so who owned the gaddi, and Haruko, there were three other craftsmen in the room, working silently. Haruko got up, dusted the ashes from her hands and wiped them carefully on her cotton scarf. She slid into the seat near the furnace and drew a lac plate to herself. There were elaborately etched gold pieces affixed to it. These were parts of a gold bracelet she was working on, one of the tasks assigned to her by Madanji. She had engraved a dancing peacock on the bracelet, a traditional motif in the elaborate jewellery craft of Jaipur, but the variations were her own. The peacock had an elongated neck and a curving crest, its train flowed like a Japanese fan. Madanji had approved, conditionally: 'You can be an excellent chitera, a master engraver, but you want to do everything, be everyone, the ghadiya, the jadiya and the enameller.' He had shaken his head at the peculiarity of the foreign girl who had come so far to be tutored in the jewellery craft his family had practised for generations.

Haruko picked the long, sharp takua and began the painstaking task of filling brilliant glass enamel into the grooves of the design. It was this traditional enamel work – meenakari – of colours that brightened in fire which had brought her to Jaipur in the first place. She was looking for a suitable project after completing her programme at the design school back in New York. She had spent a semester in Belgium the previous year, completing a gem evaluation certification and had become interested in European enamels. *Would she like to explore the Indian enamel?* her advisor had asked. *It is very interesting, both the technique and the tradition.* She had lent Haruko books on the history of enamel work and Indian jewellery craft. The brighter-hued and elaborate Indian enamel, worked in the intricate champlevé style had fascinated Haruko. Her advisor had introduced her to Madanji, a fourth-generation goldsmith, over the phone. *I have been to his shop in the bazaar*, the professor had told her. *You'll find it all very different from the European jewellery units. The bazaar's back lanes are a network of tiny manufactories, all ornaments are completely handcrafted.* The professor had smiled. *It's your type, I think you will like it.*

She did.

The first few days, Madanji had shown Haruko around the narrow alleys of the jewellers' market in the old walled city. He had introduced her to the master artisans who each practised one particular craft of stone setting or engraving or beadwork, and worked for commissioning jewellers like him. 'But there are no sunars like my grandfather any more,' he had boasted. Nandramji, Madanji's grandfather, was goldsmith to the kings. Stories of him crafting perfectly fitting bracelets and waistbands for veiled princesses, off measurements taken from their shadows falling on the floor and walls of audience rooms, were part of ornament makers' lore. When he died, princes had come to condole with the family, and the royal women had sent some of the choicest pieces of their jewellery in memoriam. A few of the necklaces and bracelets were still displayed at the gaddi. Haruko admired the scheme and symmetry of the heavy, elaborate timaniyas and pahunchis, though crafting and wearing them would be difficult now.

Haruko filled the white enamel carefully in the background of the engraved prancing peacock. Each colour of the enamel needed to be fired separately before the next one could be applied. White was the most fire resistant of all and, therefore, was the first to be applied and fired. When she finished, she placed the pieces of the bracelet carefully in the drawer of her desk for firing later, together with the pieces being crafted by other craftsmen. She raised her head and slowly rolled her shoulders. Her throat was parched, her cotton shirt had dark sweat patches on the back and front. It was the end of March and the dry heat was unlike anything Haruko had experienced. Someone had turned on a small TV, mounted high up on the wall on an improvised wooden frame. Its sounds and bright pictures disturbed Haruko. She glanced outside. The sky visible above the arched entrance of Madanji's gaddi was blue, glowing with the brilliance of the early summer sun, shining somewhere high up, just out of sight. The narrow street itself, spotted with cowpats and dog turds, was shaded, the close-leaning, tall havelis on either side keeping the sun out.

She checked the time. It was past noon, time for her to work on her own project piece, a Rajasthani hansuli – a hollow, lac-filled collar necklace decorated with enamel-and-stone work. She was setting the stones under Munnaji's supervision. Munnaji was Madanji's cousin and had his gaddi a few doors down the street. He was a top artisan, a kundansaaz who specialized in setting uncut diamonds and other stones in the purest of gold. Unlike Madanji, who knew the craft of a goldsmith but spent most of his time managing orders and commissioning work from other craftsmen, Munnaji was a pure artist – he was immersed in his delicate and difficult work from morning to evening. His gaddi was a haven of silence, no TV or music or noise of any kind. His front door always stood open at an angle, enough to allow the daylight in, but at the same time screening the interior of the shop from the street, creating an illusion of quiet seclusion in the heart of the bazaar. Munnaji had taken a liking to Haruko. Where other artisans showed her their craft because Madanji instructed them to, he did so with delight, taking pleasure in her attention, quick grasp and feather-light touch, a must for a kundansaaz working with fragile things.

'The white enamel's done. It can be fired with that kalangi.' Haruko pointed to the turban ornament a young craftsman was soldering together. 'I'd like to work on the hansuli for a couple of hours now. I am beginning to get the hang of kundan work.'

'Munnaji has a free desk for you?' Madanji asked, glancing at his ringing mobile phone. Haruko nodded. 'Meghji from the bazaar,' he exclaimed. Meghji owned the largest jewellery establishment in the main bazaar and was an important customer of Madanji's. 'Okay, okay. Go,' Madanji mouthed as he answered the phone.

Haruko retrieved a velvet case from the shoulder bag lying next to her desk and rose. She was making her project piece entirely by hand, right from pulling the gold sheets to casting the mould. She had completed engraving and enamelling it. She had chosen the single-colour technique for the enamel work and had mixed the oxide powders with fine-ground glass to produce a startling shade of lime-green. Madanji did not approve of the colour. 'The traditional colours of meena are red, blue, green,' he had said. 'Or white and black. They've been good enough for hundreds of years, for countless pieces of jewellery. I have seen newer artisans use colours like pink and turquoise blue, but yours is very strange,' he had said, turning the corners of his mouth down. However, as Madanji had explained to his enameller who was scandalized by the gleaming green enamel, it was her independent project, she had paid for the metal and the stones and worked on it by herself, a couple of hours a day, without interfering with her tasks at the gaddi.

Madanji had taken Haruko on as a favour to an American lady who visited sometimes and wrote in magazines about the goldsmiths of Johari Bazaar. Her references brought paying customers from foreign lands to his gaddi every tourist season. *I'm sending one of my students to you, to learn your wonderful art,* she had said and he had accepted. Had he known that the student was a girl when he had agreed to the unpaid apprenticeship, he would have found an excuse to turn her down. Everyone knew that women were not allowed to learn the craft of goldsmiths and artisans. However, it was too late by the time he had discovered her gender. Haruko had arrived at his haveli with a large bag strapped to her back. *It is a matter of a few weeks*, he had explained to his artisans. *She won't last*. To his astonishment, Haruko had not only lasted, she had turned out very well too, learning the different crafts quickly, completing assigned jobs without spoiling any of the pieces – something Madanji was worried about initially. She had seemed too strong, too forceful for jewellery making, which required lightness, patience. Besides, and for this Madanji was secretly even more thankful, she always dressed properly in long-sleeved shirts and baggy trousers. He had been worried about her turning up in skirts or, worse, in a pair of shorts as he had seen foreign tourists do.

Haruko stepped out into the open courtyard, strapped on the thick-soled sandals she wore everywhere, and walked out into the lane. The lane, though tucked away in one of the backstreets of Johari Bazaar, was a famous one. It boasted of shops dating back a hundred years that sold the city's favourite snacks. Haruko breathed in the piquant smells of fried savouries mingled with urine and dried cow dung as she walked to the little shack at the end of the street which sold cold drinks out of a large icebox that barely fit inside the flimsy wooden structure. She bought frosted bottles of mineral water and a can of Coke, drinking it in hurried gulps as she retraced her steps to Munnaji's gaddi. She tapped gently at the half-open wooden door. 'Come, come,' Munnaji called from the shadowed interior. Slipping off her sandals, Haruko stepped in. 'Namaste,' she joined her palms and bowed, combining the Indian and Japanese greetings. She had grown up in New York, and her mother's attempts at teaching her complicated Japanese etiquette had not succeeded beyond deep bows. Munnaji smiled broadly, 'All ready. Waiting. There,' and pointed to the wooden desk in the corner furthest from the door, laid out with a large silver bowl and two boxes, each marked with a large 'H'. They contained the purified kundan gold, uncut diamonds and other stones she was to work with.

Haruko slid behind the desk and picked up the wooden, pestle-like polishing tool. There was a large agate, the size of a dollar, set into its base. Taking a thin strip of silver, she began polishing it, passing the smooth agate over and over the piece of silver until it shone like tinsel. She took an oval-shaped diamond, transparent like glass, from one of the boxes, and measured its diameter with her callipers. Then, notching the silver strip, she cut out a piece according to the measurement and curved it into a minuscule bowl. She placed the diamond into it, the thin disk of the stone glowing white with the polished silver backing, and set it gently in the centre of one of the enamelled flowers on the necklace. She drew out a wafer-thin gold foil with a pair of fine forceps and began the careful task of inserting it into the gap between the stone and the lac-filled setting. Numerous layers of the gold foil would need to be inserted with a feather touch so as not to damage the enamel or the lac, until a gleaming raised line of gold outlined the stone. It was slow work, requiring concentration, and Munnaji set no more than twenty or twenty-five stones in one workday. Haruko's collar needed over fifty stones and she estimated that, in the time she could spare from her apprenticeship at Madanji's, it would take her about a month to complete the settings. She did not mind the time taken or the slowness of the task. The careful precision appealed to her. From time to time, Munnaji glanced up from the piece he was working on to check how she was getting along. Unlike Madanji, who had been handling foreign clients for a long time and spoke passable English, Munnaji's English was limited and he guided Haruko mainly by showing her the right way. After an hour or so, Haruko finished setting the diamond and held out the necklace to Munnaji. He took it, smiling, and placed it on the soft cloth spread on his desk. Picking up a thin sliver of the kundan gold with his silver forceps, he inserted it around the polki diamond with infinite care and the gentlest touch. Still smiling, he handed the necklace back to Haruko and she bent over the ornament again. If the kundan was not packed tightly, the stone would come loose and fall, earning disgrace for the artisan. When Munnaji was finally satisfied with her work, he took a small slab made of lac and sand and rubbed the gold setting until it glowed sun-yellow. Haruko watched the delicate strokes closely. When he finished, she replaced the collar in its velvet case and placed it on Munnaji's desk. 'Please keep it for me,' she said, pointing to the iron safe next to Munnaji's desk. 'I will return tomorrow. I am not ready to work alone yet.'

Out on the street the shadows had deepened. Haruko glanced at her watch and realized that she had been longer than intended. She bent to do up the straps of her dusty sandals. There was a sudden rushing sound, like a drum beating a tattoo, and before she knew it, she was flung violently aside. An unbearable weight descended on her legs momentarily. She heard a crunching sound. *So this is what a cracking bone sounds like,* she thought before the shadows around her turned opaque.

WHEN SHE OPENED her eyes, the jerky movement and the sound of a bleating horn told her she was in a vehicle. The pain in her body was like a heavy, tight vice. She turned her head slightly and met Madanji's anxious eyes. 'It's okay, hospital in five minutes only, nothing to worry, nothing at all. The bastard trampled you, but nothing to worry.' Munnaji gently broke open the seal of a bottle of water and put it to her mouth. The vehicle – it was an ambulance with a siren that sounded like a yapping puppy – came to a stop. Munnaji jumped out and was immediately lost in the crowded hospital. He returned shortly, with two men in white uniforms carrying a stretcher trolley. They lifted Haruko on to it. Pain and nausea swept over her. She threw up the water she had drunk. Madanji urged the stretcher bearers to hurry along.

The large casualty ward was chaotic and airless, filled with people, cries of pain, the indescribable stench of sweat, blood and disinfectants. Haruko was drenched in perspiration. She felt her lungs expand and contract painfully in an effort to draw in air. A young doctor approached.

'What happened?' he asked, deftly sifting through Haruko's body, taking inventory of pulse, temperature, injuries.

'A bull, Doctor Saab ... Someone must have thrown a stone or annoyed it, or perhaps it was only the heat ... It just rushed over her. It is God's mercy she wasn't gored, such sharp horns he had...' Madanji spoke quickly. 'Is she okay, Doctor Saab?'

'She clearly has fractures, possibly bad. The good thing is they are safe, the skin is not broken. Do you know her?'

'Yes, Doctor Saab,' Madanji said. 'She is from outside, from Amreeka. She is learning our work, making jewellery. We are teaching her...'

'Very good, very fantastic,' Munnaji added, pointing to Haruko, his eyes fixed on her face.

'Okay. One of you will need to fill the form for her. Luckily, the senior resident for orthopaedics is on his rounds.' He asked the nurse who was cleaning Haruko's bruises to fetch a syringe. 'Miss,' he turned to Haruko, 'I am going to give you something to ease the pain by injection now. You might feel a bit drowsy. We will also take X-rays. The senior resident will need to see them.'

Haruko tried to speak but her throat was dry, constricted. Munnaji accompanied her as she was wheeled down a long corridor. His concerned eyes were the last thing she saw before she drifted away. She was jolted into consciousness by a shrill cry, as pain rose like flames over her. Sweat poured from every pore and she trembled uncontrollably. *I did not know I could scream like that*, she thought, as she ground her teeth together.

'I am sorry, it won't hurt now. I had to move your leg to suspend it so I can apply the plaster securely.' A tall man was standing over her, twisting the lid off a small box. Light from somewhere glinted off his spectacles. She could not see his eyes, but his voice was calming. 'I promise there won't be any more pain,' he said absently, as he pulled out what looked like a blue roll of bandage from the box. With astonishing rapidity and skill, he began applying the bandage from ankle to knee, occasionally wetting his gloved hands with water from a bowl held out by the nurse. 'It is very important to keep this leg stabilized,' he said, giving the rapidly drying plaster a final pat. 'The fibula is broken in two places and the tibia has a crack as well. But you've been lucky – there is no dislocation. Eight weeks of immobilization and you'll be okay.'

Haruko looked at her leg. Bright blue and suspended above her, it hardly seemed a part of her body.

'I can admit you here,' the doctor continued, 'but it might be difficult to find a room, and you see the state the wards are in.' He waved his hand. 'Besides, they will keep your leg strapped up and suspended like this the whole time. So if you think you can rest the leg and be good by yourself, I can let you go home.'

'Very good, very fantastic,' chimed in Munnaji, hovering somewhere out of the range of Haruko's sight.

'I will follow your instructions.' She cleared her dry throat. 'But I live on the third floor and there is no elevator...'

'Third floor?' the doctor raised his eyebrows. 'Impossible. You cannot climb stairs at all for weeks.'

'No worry, Doctor Saab. Munnaji has very good room with no stairs. She will stay there, no worry at all.' Madanji had joined them by now.

'Okay. Very good. You'll need to come back in a week's time for check-up.' The doctor peeled off the rubber surgical gloves, stained blue from the bandage, and tossed them in the bin by the side of the bed. He paused. 'You are Japanese?'

Haruko nodded. It was simpler to say yes.

'My fiancée is in Japan, on a research fellowship at the topmost university there.' He smiled for the first time. 'Come next week at around eleven, and I will see you myself.' Haruko saw that his eyes were large and clear, the brown irises shining with calm light. 'And remember, complete bed rest. No movement of the leg at all,' he said and walked away.

MUNNAJI'S HAVELI WAS a street away from Madanji's home. Haruko was brought into the front room on a stretcher. The women of Munnaji's family, his wife, sister, daughters, whom

Haruko had never met before, clustered around her, clucking and commiserating. Munnaji's youngest daughter, Leela, a quiet girl of perhaps thirteen, took charge of Haruko. She fetched warm water and a towel and, closing the door of the room, helped Haruko out of her torn and bloodied clothes. She dipped the towel in warm water and wiped Haruko down thoroughly, handling her bruised body with practised gentleness. Choosing a loose cotton kimono from Haruko's clothes, she helped her put it on.

'You are very good at this, Leela,' Haruko remarked.

Leela smiled, 'Last year Dadi-sa very sick. I look after her every day. I give good massage too, I massage her in the winters when her legs hurt.'

Later that night and every night for the weeks Haruko was not allowed to move about unaided, Leela slept on a cotton mattress spread on the floor beside Haruko's bed.

Haruko was to learn that the haveli was Munnaji's maternal home. His mother had died in childbirth and his maternal grandfather, a renowned kundansaaz who did not have any sons of his own, had adopted him. He grew up in this house where the mother he had never seen had been born and had lived until womanhood, cared for by one of his mother's sisters, a young childless widow. He called her Ma-sa and she now lived with his family, honoured as his mother. He learned his adoptive father's craft and turned out to be a worthy successor to his famed gaddi, the undisputed number-one kundansaaz in the bazaar.

Haruko was given the baithak, or the outer room belonging to the men of the family and their male visitors, instead of a room inside because it had a newly built bathroom attached to it. It faced away from the larger of the haveli's two courtyards and had a covered entrance leading into the street. In order to make the room private for Haruko, a printed bed sheet was hung at the entrance. The women of Madanji's family – his wife, mother, three daughters and a married sister who was visiting – occupied inner rooms which opened into the chandani, the smaller inner courtyard. She was, however, never left alone. Leela was with her most of the time. Every morning, before leaving for school, she brought a bucket of lukewarm water, poured a tablespoon of coconut oil and lemon juice in it, and sponged her, applied medicated ointments to her cuts and bruises, and made her bed. She brought Haruko her breakfast – a glass of milk with turmeric and dates, some sweet, rich porridge, thick homemade potato chips and savouries.

'The morning stuff is a lot of trouble for you,' Haruko said one afternoon as Leela was doing her homework on the floor beside her bed. She knew that Leela had been late for school that day and had left with a hurried mouthful of porridge and her long braid unkempt.

'No trouble, Jiji. I was lazy this morning. If I wake up early, I don't get remark for untidiness at school.'

While Leela was at school, the women of the family trickled in and out of the baithak. Munnaji's mother came every morning after praying at the temple in the main bazaar and fed Haruko the tulsi leaves and sugar crystals offered to the gods. His wife and sisters unrolled cotton carpets beside her bed and picked pulses, chopped vegetables, kneaded dough. Besides Leela, none of them spoke English, but they conveyed their concern and friendliness through broad smiles, vigorous nods and glasses of spiced milk. Haruko had never had so many people around her. The goings and comings, and the continuous flow of activity were oddly soothing. She felt like she was living in a richly coloured picture book.

Haruko spent her days in bed, resting, reading, listening to music and chatting with Leela. Leela had fetched all of Haruko's books from the third-floor eyrie in Madanji's house. Among them were her old textbooks on design, illustrated with architectural drawings, pictures and plates of gorgeous ornaments, of her own work and those of others, at the design school. Leela was curious about them. She took to leafing through the books after finishing her schoolwork, poring over pictures of projects Haruko had completed. She asked questions about the ornaments, noticed the differences between them and the jewellery craft she saw all around her, and marvelled at the drawings in Haruko's sketchbooks. Haruko found herself talking to her about the basic concepts of design, proportions and harmony, contrast and asymmetry, lines and colour. She showed Leela how to use her drawing instruments, and set simple tasks for her to complete – sections of books to read, or drawings to copy. Leela stumbled on technical terms and often couldn't follow the English. Haruko patiently explained. She stressed the importance of learning the actual craft of making ornaments.

'Drawing and learning from books only takes you so far, it's the ornament makers who are the real deal.'

'So the work of sunars is important like that of designers, Jiji?' Leela asked.

'Absolutely. There's nothing more important than being a sunar. You are not a jewellery designer unless you can craft what you have imagined.'

Almost a week after Haruko's accident, Munnaji returned earlier than usual from his gaddi accompanied by a skinny man, one of the runners who ran errands in the lanes, carrying a work desk. The desk was placed near the entrance to the baithak such that Haruko had a clear view of it from her bed. Munnaji unrolled a cotton floor seat beside the desk and smiled broadly at Haruko, saying, 'I work here. You watch and learn.' He was soon engrossed in his work. She watched closely until the tears in her eyes blurred the detailed setting Munnaji was working on.

Haruko had texted her professor and her father about the accident. *A fracture, not serious,* she had written. Her father had responded to her message promptly, asking whether she had good medical care. *Make sure the doctors know what they are doing, and don't worry about money, I'll wire whatever's needed*, he had texted. Her professor has replied too. *Don't worry, you'll be fine, best time to think and visualize now that you are forced to be still. Tell me how it goes, don't hesitate to ask for help*, she had said.

Haruko had considered but decided against informing her mother. She could have left a message at the psychiatric facility her mother had been a patient at for the past several years. She knew that the staff there read messages out to inmates during group therapy sessions. She had left messages for her in the past, to mark occasions or to tell her about events in her life – her graduation, her break-up with her high-school boyfriend, her acceptance at the famous design school, seeing the Japan Sea for the first time. Gradually, she had stopped. There was never any reply.

By the time Haruko had reached high school, her mother had begun slipping away to live in a time and place somewhere in her memory. During those periods, she would wander through their suburban home in New Jersey, singing Japanese songs, picking flowers in an imaginary meadow and holding a child visible only to her. She was unable to recognize her husband, would call Haruko by unfamiliar names and endearments. Gradually, the periods of wandering increased and she began speaking only in Japanese, cooking only Japanese food. She cycled in the neighbourhood, sometimes for hours on end, while Haruko and her father were away during the day. On occasion, neighbours and community workers had to escort her home, dirt-stained and tired, bruised and bleeding from a fall. Just before Haruko's graduation from high school, they had been forced to admit her to an institution for mental illness. Her father had received a call from the police station while at work. She had been cycling in the middle of the expressway among speeding cars. It was a miracle she hadn't been run over, the police officer had said. He had to take the day off from work and drive to the police station to fetch her. At home, Haruko's mother had sat on the sofa cradling her in her arms, cooing to her in mellifluous Japanese, while her father spoke over the phone to the hospital, making arrangements for her admission. Haruko had laid her head on her mother's shoulder, curled her long legs, and allowed herself to be rocked in the warm circle of her arms. A couple of days later, her father had driven her mother to the hospital. She had held a small bag of nightclothes and toiletries on her lap and had glanced unseeingly at Haruko as the car turned out of the driveway. Initially, Haruko went every weekend to see her, took walks with her in the walled garden of the hospital, and chatted to her, telling her about her school, her friends. Her mother always seemed sleepy, vague. She seldom spoke, and when she did it was always to a child who was not Haruko. Then she was moved to a psychiatric facility farther away. Haruko herself went away too, first to college and later to the design school in New York, and hardly ever saw her mother. Her father receded too. He sold the home Haruko had grown up in and where they had lived together as a family, and bought an apartment closer to his work. He became an enthusiastic golfer and went away for golfing weekends. Haruko hadn't seen him since her graduation day, which he had dutifully attended, taking her out to lunch at a Korean restaurant afterwards.

MADANJI CALLED A taxi and accompanied Haruko for her hospital appointment a week later.

At the hospital, Haruko waited in a wheelchair at the crowded outpatient department while Madanji made inquiries about the orthopaedic clinic.

'Hello, it's a week, is it? You are here for your check-up?' The senior resident from last time was standing beside her.

'Yes, Madanji is checking for an appointment.'

'Appointment? There are no appointments. The OPD is always overflowing.' The doctor glanced around at the crowd in the large hall. 'Go into casualty. I'll see you there in some time.'

Madanji had joined them by now. 'Will it take long, Doctor Saab?' he asked hesitatingly.

'It might. I think we'll need an X-ray before the examination. Only after the examination will I be able to tell whether we need anything further like a CT, etc.'

Madanji's face fell – there was work to be done at the gaddi. 'I have two foreign customers coming this afternoon,' he said.

'You can go. I will arrange for an ambulance to take her back,' the doctor said and motioned to an orderly. 'Take her to the duty doctors' room in casualty.'

'I can take a taxi,' Haruko said as the orderly wheeled her away, but the doctor and Madanji had already walked off.

The duty doctors' room adjoining the crowded casualty ward was brightly lit. It was furnished with a bed, several wooden chairs and a writing table. The window air-conditioner, too big for the room's proportions, hissed like a blowtorch. A young man in a crumpled doctor's apron was fast asleep in one of the chairs, and another was drinking tea. He raised his eyebrows as Haruko was wheeled into the room and the orderly answered the unspoken question: 'Doctor Saab told me to bring Madam here.'

A door to the left opened, and a woman doctor emerged towelling her face dry. 'These forty-eight-hour duties are killers. I'll do the rounds of the ward now, you two sleep.' Her gaze fell on Haruko.

'Boss has sent her to wait here,' the tea-drinking doctor said.

'Fracture? Here for a check-up?' the woman doctor asked. Haruko nodded. 'You've got reports?' Haruko handed her the hospital folder with her reports. She extracted the X-ray and held it up towards the electric light. 'Pretty bad. This one's a week old, you'll need another X-ray to check progress. You'll need to go to the radiology department for that. Anyone with you?'

'No,' Haruko said, 'but I can go by myself.'

'You'll get lost,' the doctor laughed. Drops of water gleaming like diamonds fell from her hair. 'Sister!' she called. A nurse entered. 'Ask Mangilalji to take her for an X-ray.' She scribbled a note and handed it to Haruko. 'If all's well in the X-ray, perhaps a CT won't be needed,' she said and stepped out of the room.

As the orderly wheeled her through the ward towards the radiology department, Haruko saw her bending over a wailing child with both legs encased in bloodstained bandages.

With the note from the doctor and the orderly's hustling, Haruko's X-ray did not take long. After the X-ray, the orderly brought Haruko back to the doctors' room. The room was now empty but the overhead lights still blazed brightly and the air conditioner was switched on. Haruko took a sketchbook out of her shoulder bag and began sketching a pale gecko clinging to the blue ceiling of the room, its tail curled, its body glowing translucent. She was doing a third sketch of the gecko, the body foreshortened and the curled tail elongated, when the senior resident entered.

'Sorry it took so long. Have you got the X-ray?'

Haruko handed it over and strapped her sketchbook shut. The doctor called a nurse to help Haruko on to the bed. He studied the X-ray carefully and then examined her leg, tapping her knee and flexing the toes.

'Everything looks okay. The plaster's in good condition and the X-ray shows no abnormal change. Next week, same time.'

He turned to the nurse, 'Call for an ambulance,' then asked Haruko, 'To the old city, right?'

'Yes, but I would really prefer a taxi. Besides, it is past lunchtime and I am hungry. I'd like to stop on the way to grab a bite.'

'That would mean walking. Your leg can't take any weight yet.' The doctor glanced at his watch. 'There's a canteen here, decent food. I haven't had lunch either.'

The canteen was a cavernous hall with tables and chairs strewn all over. The orderly wheeled Haruko to one of the round plastic tables. The doctor scanned the menu scribbled in white chalk on a rusty old blackboard.

'There are burgers and noodles. I am ordering dal chawal for myself. It is one of the staple meals and quite good here.'

'Sure. I like dal chawal too,' Haruko replied.

The doctor cast a curious glance at her and, summoning a waiter, ordered two thalis. The smoke-darkened kitchen was visible from where they sat. Sweaty men in undershirts were chopping vegetables, kneading dough, stirring large pots.

While they waited for the food, Haruko told him about her work. 'Do you think I could start? I don't need to move much, my work's done sitting on the floor.'

'You are already getting bored alone?'

'I am not alone at all. There are people around constantly, Munnaji's family. But I have a schedule to keep to and my project to complete. If I do not finish on time, everything else will get pushed back.'

'I see. You can work if you feel well enough to, but you must keep your leg elevated and tension free. Mild elevation's fine. Place a small cushion or pillow under the leg. If the leg hurts or feels heavy, you must increase the elevation and rest it.'

The food arrived in steel trays. Haruko inhaled the special fragrance of boiled rice, garnished lentils and pickled lemon. She mixed the rice with the yellow lentils and crumbled crisp papad on to the mixture.

The doctor laughed. 'You know how to eat like a Marwari!'

'I have been here six months.' Haruko smiled. 'I love this food!' She bit into the pickle.

'That's very spicy! I thought Japanese people can't handle spices. At least my fiancée's friend can't. She ate some savoury snack and her eyes watered. My fiancée said she was quite worried for a while, the way her friend gasped and coughed.'

'I am only part Japanese, my father's Korean. I grew up eating kimchi for snacks. I can take you on, chilli for chilli!'

'So you are from Korea, not Japan?'

'It's not that simple. My father was born in the US, he met my Japanese mother in Japan while working at the American base there. I was born in Hong Kong and grew up in New York. I speak no Korean and have never been to Korea. On the other hand, I speak Japanese fluently, I have travelled from one end of Japan to the other, attended tea ceremonies, watched bunraku, and I love manga. I have even tried to learn playing the samisen. The only Japanese thing I haven't done is attend a cherry-viewing party!'

'So you are kind of Japanese.'

'Yeah,' Haruko agreed. 'Kind of is about right. Is your fiancée enjoying Japan?'

'A bit too much I think. She has been delaying her return. She has put it off three times now. The professors there like her, she has always been good at studies, always stood first since her school days.'

'You must be very proud of her.'

The doctor signalled to the waiter for a second helping of dal. 'Well, despite her good academic record, she opted for literature and sociology in high school and college.' He shook his head. 'If her parents were strict, she would have taken science. She would have passed the entrance exam for medicine and would be a qualified doctor by now, like her elder sister. But she told them she couldn't imagine seeing sick people every day, all her life.'

'There's something to be said for that. Anyway, it can't be good for both of you to be in the same profession.' Haruko smiled. 'It might get boring.'

'No, no,' the doctor said earnestly. 'It would have been very good. I am working here at the government hospital only for a few years. I have plans to set up my own clinic. She could have practised with me. Many of my batchmates have married doctors.'

'Why didn't you?'

He looked at her in surprise. 'How could I? Our families have had an understanding for years.' He ate in silence for some time. 'And it's not so bad. She won't have to be away on night duty or emergency calls. She will probably teach at the university and have plenty of time for family. So I think it will work out well, overall.' Pushing his tray aside, he took out his phone. 'This is her, third from the right. I took this on Diwali, right before she left for Japan.'

Haruko looked at the girl in the picture, dressed in a pink bodice and a shimmering, flowing skirt. She was slight, her wide eyes looked away at something beyond the lens of the camera, her lips were slightly parted. 'She is very pretty. You are a lucky man, Doctor.'

The doctor smiled. 'Yes, my batchmates say so too – that I am lucky to have found someone like her.'

Haruko finished her meal and wiped her fingers as well as she could on the rough paper napkin. The orderly, who had been idling about, chatting with the waiters, now came forward.

'Where exactly in the walled city do you need to go?' the doctor asked.

'To the goldsmith's lane, just off the main jeweller's market. It is behind the street with a lot of old shops selling savouries. It is quite famous, I am told. '

'Of course. I know Namkeenvalon ki Gali – excellent savoury shops, the best in the entire city. Actually, I am off duty now. I can drop you and buy some savouries for home from there.'

'That's too much trouble for you. I'll be quite all right in a cab...' Haruko began.

'No, no, it's nothing.'

The doctor drove a newish sedan. Its interiors smelt of air freshener and air conditioning. He drove slowly, honking frequently.

'This is a nice car,' Haruko said. 'I have only been in old Ambassador taxis since I've been here. And that smelly ambulance, of course.'

The doctor looked straight ahead. 'My parents bought it for me when I completed my post-graduate specialization. I'll have a new one soon. My fiancée's parents are planning to buy a new car for us for the wedding.'

'I thought you said she had postponed her return?'

'Yes, but she will return in a month in any case. I'll complete my MCH in a few months too. Life will become a bit easier. I won't have these forty-eight-hour duties.'

'And has she finished her research work?'

'I think some part remains, but she can finish it here. She's been there long enough, almost three years.'

They were crossing the crowded bazaar now. There were cycle rickshaws and scooters and three-wheeled auto rickshaws zigzagging and cutting lanes without warning. 'This place is a mess.' The doctor honked repeatedly, his shoulders tense. They turned slowly into the lane named for the savoury shops lining it on both sides. Every shop displayed mounds of golden snacks of every shape and size, from crisp sev to thick knots of ganthiya. Fried almonds and cashews, roasted and spiced peanuts and chickpeas were heaped up in large platters. Bunches of people stood in the street, tasting, buying, eating from paper cones. The doctor honked in vain to clear a path for the car.

Haruko glanced at his tense face, rolled down the window on her side and leaned out. 'O bhaya!' she called out, hailing the people just as she had seen Madanji do. Several heads turned in their direction, people stared, laughed and moved aside to make way for the car to pass.

The doctor cast a sidelong look at her. 'You have become quite the local.'

'I have to be. I am learning jewellery craft from the people who live in these streets.'

'Learning? But you said you studied in New York. What can these illiterate sunars teach you?'

'A lot. They are phenomenal artists, some of them.'

'Artists? The sunars?'

'Yes, these ornament makers. You should see their work. They are true artists.' She pointed to a haveli painted pink and green. 'That's my home for the time being. Isn't it lovely?' The doctor halted the car. Munnaji was already at work in the entranceway. 'Thanks so much. I really brought you out of your way.'

'No, no, don't mention it. Is this a sunar's shop as well?'

'No, Munnaji's gaddi is one street away, but he's been working here in the evenings since my accident. He knows that I can learn by observing him, so he works where I can see him. He knows it is important for me to continue my lessons,' Haruko smiled. 'Only a true artist knows the importance of his art.' Leela and her elder sisters hurried down the steps to help Haruko out. 'If you have time, do come in.'

'Some other time. I haven't been home for two days. I will see you next week. Come straight to the duty doctors' room. If anyone asks, say Dr Prakash has asked you to wait there. And remember, no weight on that leg.'

Haruko got out of the car, leaning on Leela's shoulder. The gold and red of the setting sun fell on the even plains of her smooth, pale face. 'I am Haruko Shin. Thanks for today, Prakash.'

THE NEXT DAY, Leela returned from school and found Haruko propped up in bed, surrounded by sketchbooks, pencil cases and unfamiliar-looking instruments. Leela clicked her tongue, 'Jiji, you will get pain in your back.' She brought long, round bolster pillows and arranged them around her. Only when she was certain of Haruko's comfort, did she take out her schoolbooks.

While Leela finished her homework, Haruko looked through her old sketchbooks. She propped one on a cushion in her lap and began sketching the flowers and vines, peacocks and parrots that adorned the walls and ceilings of the baithak. Leela watched her with quiet attention. Then, opening her notebook at the back, she began copying the designs too.

Munnaji found the two of them drawing busily that evening. He smiled happily and repeated 'very good, very fantastic' several times, nodding to himself, before taking his place at his desk.

The next evening, he brought home another work desk and arranged the velvet case of the hansuli and boxes of gold leaf and stones on it. Haruko raised herself gingerly on her crutches and hopped on one leg to the desk. Leela adjusted the floor seat so that Haruko could lean against the wall and placed a pillow under her knee. Haruko picked up the fine forceps, her grip firm and light, and began working carefully.

FOR THE NEXT check-up, Madanji came to fetch her in a taxi. Haruko insisted on going by herself. She was much stronger, she said, and she knew the hospital and the doctor. 'I will be fine, really,' she said, slinging her bag on her shoulder.

Madanji looked guiltily relieved, a hospital visit meant the loss of most of the working day. He instructed the taxi driver to be very careful. 'Don't drive the car like a horse carriage, the foreign lady is injured.'

At the hospital, Haruko clamped the crutches firmly under her arms, and taking care to hold her injured leg above the ground, hobbled through the crowds milling in the wide entrance hall. Several long corridors, dimly lit by daylight filtering through dust-encrusted windows, branched off from the hall. Haruko recalled turning left last time, but was soon lost in the maze of wards. She wandered through the corridors filled with people lying on pallets on the floor, whole families squatting in corners and under staircases, children running about, women nursing babies, old people coughing and spitting. And through the chaos, doctors and nurses walked rapidly, seldom stopping at the groans and entreaties from the crowds.

By the time she found her way to the duty doctors' room, it was almost twelve o'clock. The room seemed frozen in time from her last visit – the electric lights blazed bright, one doctor lay fast asleep, another was drinking tea, the gecko was still on the blue ceiling.

The tea drinker raised his head, there were dark moons of exhaustion under his eyes. 'Boss was waiting for you here, he has gone to the ortho ward now. He said he'll be back after his round. You are to wait here.' He pointed to a chair and, rising wearily, left the room.

Haruko settled in the chair and took out her sketchbook to continue working on the design of a flower-shaped ornament she had begun the day before.

By the time Dr Prakash returned, the sleeping doctor had woken up and left as well, and Haruko was alone. She was carefully drawing a cross-section view of the flower.

'You were late,' he said briskly and called a nurse. 'Get a ward boy, we'll need an X-ray and I want to see if anything needs to be done about the plaster.'

'I lost my way getting here. This place is vast, and the crowds are unbelievable.'

'Lost? What do you mean? Was no one with you?'

'No, I came by myself today.'

'That was very unwise.' The doctor frowned. 'Your leg is in no shape for so much walking and strain.'

'It's okay, I am not a kid! I was careful. I used my crutches and did not put any weight on it.'

'We shall see. The X-ray will reveal everything.' He motioned for her to get into the wheelchair the ward boy had brought.

The X-ray was all right and Prakash had to admit that the cast was fine too. He was impressed. 'No dirt at all. It is very clean.'

'Of course it is! I wipe it down with a wet tissue every night. Remember, I am kind of Japanese!' Prakash smiled. 'Also I have worked every day on my project. I think I will complete it on time.'

'That's very good, very impressive. It is all a matter of how disciplined you are. Not everyone is as disciplined, you know. You've had lunch?'

'Munnaji's wife packed some food.' Haruko extracted a large cardboard box from her bag. 'In fact, there's enough for two. Munnaji's wife makes delicious parathas.' She rose from the wheelchair.

'Don't get up, don't get up. I will pull the table closer.'

Haruko opened the box and the room became redolent with the smells of ghee and pickles. She squeezed some hand sanitizer on to her hands and offered the tube to Prakash. 'You see, I came prepared!'

They ate with their fingers, and Haruko spoke about her project. 'I've made up for lost time. I am my own mistress now, since Madanji is not giving me work. I guess he is worried about liability!'

'Liability? What liability?'

'In the US, you'd be sued if you made a sick employee work. You've got to pay them and let them stay at home.'

'If we do that here, we'll lose half the workforce of the hospital. We work even when we are sick, as long as we can manage to stand upright.'

'Now that is really impressive!'

Prakash shrugged. 'It's the job. So when your project's done, what will you do? Go back to the US?'

'No, after finishing here I will go to Bombay. I like to work with the range of lesser gems, those which are not as hard as diamonds or stones of the sapphire family. I want to see how they are hand-cut and polished here. I have everything planned and must finish within two months, three at most.'

'You are very particular about keeping to schedules.'

'Yes, absolutely. Schedules are essential, they give

structure, otherwise it is easy to get too immersed and carried away, forget time and place. That's the end of all order – forgetting.'

'You are right. This is discipline. I wish my fiancée could learn some. She has postponed her return again.'

'Really? Are you sure she wants to come back?'

'Of course. She can't live in a foreign country.' Haruko looked at the troubled brown eyes behind the rimless glasses. He took a bite of the thick paratha. 'Tokyo is a big city, isn't it, very different from here?'

'Yes, it is. Big and busy, crowds everywhere. Roads and rail-lines rise in tiers, one above the other, and people live in hatbox-like apartments. Very futuristic, but also very old. It is beautiful in its own way too. Why don't you go and see for yourself? That would show your fiancée how eager you are for her to return.'

'Go to Tokyo? No, no, that's impossible. I have my exams, and interviews for teaching appointments at the medical college are coming up. No,' he repeated and shook his head decisively, 'my going to Japan is out of question. It is time for her to come back, she's been away long enough.'

They finished eating and Haruko replaced the lid on the box, securing it with colourful rubber-bands. She placed the box in her shoulder bag.

Prakash stood watching her preparations. 'If you are not in a hurry, I can drop you at the haveli. I just have a few cases to see. You can wait here.'

'Sure, that would be great. Thanks.' Haruko propped her bag on the table and took out her sketchbook and pencil case.

Prakash pushed a wooden stool close to her. 'Elevate the leg. I'll try and hurry.'

He returned after almost an hour to find her bent over the sketchbook, her leg propped on the upper rung of the stool. 'Sorry, you had to wait so long. I hope you were not bored.'

Haruko raised her head. 'Not at all. I was working. A hair ornament – sheeshphool they call it.' Her eyes slid back to her sketch.

'Very good, but that is the wrong way to elevate. You must support the ankle and the shin.' He lifted her leg and placed it straight, ankle and shin resting on the seat of the stool. 'Like this. I will send someone to wheel you to the front porch.' He strode out again.

Haruko glanced at her sketch. In the final iteration, the five-petalled flower was a mixture of an iris and a jasmine. She was not displeased with a Japanese motif seeping into the Indian ornament.

Prakash was waiting in the car, engine running, when the ward boy wheeled her out. He eased the car through the great iron gates and joined the scooters and tempos and trucks jostling for space on the broad road. The hospital was in the new part of the city, which was as crowded as the old city built by the kings, the wall built to circumscribe it almost entirely demolished. There were large diagnostic centres and pharmacies on either side of the road, and a constant ebb and flow of people. Pavements were crowded with pedestrians and juice sellers and snack vendors.

'The city is growing every day,' Prakash said, manoeuvring the car ahead of slow-moving rickshaws. 'And getting busier. Of course, not like Bombay. Or Tokyo. But it is our city, it is familiar to us. That means something, no?' Haruko looked at him. He had clear, pale skin and, despite the stubble and tired shadows, he managed to look tidy and alert. He shook his head. 'I can't understand her. She told her sister she can't leave Tokyo right now, things are not finished, it is a great place, she really likes it there ... What's wrong with here? This is the city of her birth, she's lived here all her life. Doesn't that matter? You need your own people around you, your family ... But she says she likes Tokyo now, has made friends there. As if that makes it any less foreign.' A line emerged between his thick brows.

Haruko looked away. 'Tokyo has a certain allure for sure,' she said slowly. 'And maybe it is the foreignness that is attractive to her. It can be quite powerful, foreignness...' They were driving through the main market. 'Would you mind stopping over at one of the stationery shops please? I need a couple of sketchbooks.'

Prakash stopped the car in front of a block of shops with ornate pillars and arches, all painted pink, the city's colour. 'You sit, I will get it for you.' He left the engine running and returned in a few minutes with thick, large books, garish pictures of women carrying pitchers of water against a desert sunset on the covers. 'They did not have fancy ones like yours, but these are the best available.'

'Thanks, these are great. They are for Leela. She likes to draw, and I am showing her how. I think she has an eye for detail. She will take over her father's gaddi one day.'

'Sunars don't teach jewellery making to their women. It is surprising they agreed to teach you ... Perhaps because you are a foreigner.'

'That's nonsense. I am not a foreigner among the artisans. I belong among them, just as you belong in that hospital. I can engrave and enamel and do jadav to match any of Madanji's sunars.'

'So you will rent a shop in the bazaar and set up a gaddi of your own?' Prakash asked, amused.

'Absolutely! That's the plan. I will design and craft and sell my own pieces. After Bombay, a month in Cuttack, a couple in Benares and Hyderabad, perhaps a few back in Europe, and in a couple of years, I will have sufficient pieces to open an independent studio. One of the top diamond traders – an Indian, incidentally – saw my work in Belgium and has agreed to put in some capital.'

They reached Munnaji's haveli and Prakash helped her out.

Munnaji's wife welcomed him with joined palms and spoke from behind the end of her sari to Leela.

'Mummy asking you to drink tea,' Leela conveyed in her best English.

'Come if you have time,' Haruko said. 'Their savouries are better than those sold in the shops around here.'

'If it is not inconvenient...' Prakash began.

'Inconvenient? Nothing's inconvenient for them! Haven't they been looking after an invalid stranger night and day?'

The girls bustled about fetching tea, homemade mathris and laddus, hot snacks. Leela, all smiles, brought a plastic chair for Prakash. Munnaji's wife spread a cotton mat on the floor for the rest, and urged her daughters to fill his plate.

Haruko pointed out the elegant plaster mouldings and murals on the walls and ceiling. 'Aren't these fabulous? I am copying them. Leela's doing better than me though.'

Leela blushed, handing a plate of food to Prakash.

Munnaji's aunt entered, her fingers turning prayer beads inside the small cloth bag she carried everywhere with her. She blessed Haruko and Prakash and spoke softly to Leela. 'Dadi-sa saying please make Jiji's leg better, Doctor Saab.' Leela smiled her full smile. 'She saying Jiji too beautiful to have lame leg.' The old woman raised her palm in blessing again and settled in a corner with her prayer beads.

'They've all been terrific,' Haruko said. 'I have never had so much attention in my life, or food for that matter. Endless glasses of milk with turmeric, and all sorts of porridges with homemade butter at all times.'

'That's our way here. My father teaches at the university and brings home his students for meals without any notice, and my mother cooks for them all without a word of complaint. She has pots large enough to cook for twenty-thirty people at one go.'

'Wow. She must be an angel to never complain. I would. Love's all right, but running a kitchen for hungry students is no joke. And if the students around here are anywhere near as hungry as I used be when I was at Uni, she must spend all her time in the kitchen!'

Prakash laughed. His face relaxed, and the thin line between his brows disappeared.

Shortly afterwards, Munnaji arrived from the gaddi. He smiled his broadest smile, bent his head and touched his joined palms to his forehead in greeting. The room was now full of people. They all talked to Prakash – Munnaji, his daughters, his wife too, forgetting her custom of not speaking to men directly. Haruko watched quietly, resting against the pillows.

Prakash turned to her. 'I'll be leaving now. The family were worried that you went to the hospital alone. They thought Madanji was to go with you.'

'I told him not to bother. He has a living to earn. I have travelled around the world on my own, going to the hospital is no big deal. Besides, you looked after me really well.'

'That's okay, but they are right to worry. You are their responsibility here and you've already had an accident.'

'They couldn't have done anything about the accident, unless you are saying people around here have supernatural powers and know when charging bulls will trample visiting apprentices!'

Prakash remained serious. 'I have told them you need not come to the hospital next week. I will come here and check on you. The hospital is full of secondary infections anyway, and this will be far better for your health.'

'That's crazy. I can't allow you to do that unless you take a fee.'

'Oh, they already offered to pay me and I said no. I am not allowed to practise privately. It could cost me my licence. The only problem is, I can't fix a time – you've seen how it is at the hospital. So I will come whenever I can.'

'That's hardly a problem. I am not allowed to go anywhere you know – doctor's orders!'

Prakash laughed. Munnaji's family saw him off, everyone talking until the last.

MADANJI CAME LATER that evening. Both Haruko and Munnaji were at work. Munnaji looked up from his task and spoke in a sharp tone as Madanji stood with bowed head, shuffling his feet. Then he came up to Haruko looking shamefaced and asked after her health. 'Tell me if you need any help with the hansuli.'

'Actually, the hansuli is fine. Munnaji keeps an eye on it. Yesterday, he made me reset two stones, he said they did not glow right.' Haruko laughed. 'But there is something else

I need to do.' She opened her sketchbook and showed the iris-jasmine to Madanji, front, back and cross-section views neatly sequenced and scaled.

'Sheeshphool? For head? What do you want it for? It's a bride's ornament, not common now.'

'One of the women in the mural is wearing a pair.' Haruko pointed to the wall. 'I want to make this. I can do the engraving and enamel on my own, but someone will have to fire it for me. Also the material. I need gold, enamel, a few diamonds for the dewdrops here.'

Madanji looked at the drawings, the delicate shape and fine patterns on the petals. 'It will be first rate if you can make it the way you draw it.'

'I can,' Haruko said.

THE NEXT DAY, Madanji sent over some pulled sheets of gold and Haruko worked on cutting and shaping the ornament. When Leela returned from school late in the afternoon, she was still at work.

Leela came up to her. 'Jiji, Dadi-sa sitting there all day.' She pointed to the entranceway. 'She not eating food because you not eating.'

Haruko was startled. She hadn't noticed the old woman in the entranceway. 'She's gone hungry all day? Why didn't she say anything, Leela?'

Leela didn't answer. She fetched platters of kadhi chawal

for Haruko and her grandmother and sat beside Dadi-sa who fed her mouthfuls with her fingers.

After the meal, Haruko asked Leela to bring her sketchbook. 'We will do design drawing today. I'll show you detailing and technical stuff, like scale and proportion and drawing a piece from different angles.'

Later in the evening, Munnaji stood watching the two girls. Their dark heads almost touched and they were engrossed. There were coloured pencils, dividers, set squares laid out neatly, and Leela was drawing with one of Haruko's pencils.

Haruko looked up. 'She's the real deal, Munnaji. Very good, as you say, very fantastic. Catches on like anything. She'll be terrific for your gaddi.'

Munnaji stood watching Leela, and then shook his head pensively. After he left, Leela spoke. 'Papaji saying only sons make jewellery. Girl cannot be sunar. But he is wrong. You are girl and you are become sunar, Jiji.'

'Absolutely, I am as sunar as they get. And you are one too, don't let anyone tell you differently. They'll discover it for themselves later on.' Leela smiled a full smile that transformed her demure face. Haruko reached over and squeezed her thin shoulders.

A WEEK LATER, Prakash arrived late in the afternoon. The household was asleep and Haruko was showing Leela the basic shapes in metalwork. He knocked softly.

Haruko looked up. 'Hello! I did not expect you until later. How have you been?'

'I should ask you this, you are the patient.' He smiled cautiously.

'And you should answer yourself, you are the doctor!'

Leela slipped away to rouse her sisters to boil tea and fry batches of crisp pakoras while Prakash examined Haruko.

'Everything looks fine. At this rate, you can soon begin using this leg. You must be getting bored out of your mind in this room.'

'Not at all. I am teaching Leela. And I am working on new things.' She opened her sketchbook and turned it towards him. 'Remember the bridal ornament I was drawing the other day? Which reminds me, how goes with the reluctant bride?'

Prakash examined the sketch. 'She's been told she needs to return within the next few weeks. Her father spoke to her. She must come back whether her work is finished or not, he has told her clearly.'

'And what did she say?'

'What would she say? Her father has spoken, she'll be here soon.'

'Wow. She didn't say anything at all, not even to you?'

'To me? No, no, of course not. This is between her parents and her. Anyway, everyone is going mad with preparations. I will bring the wedding card before it is finalized. I don't like any of the designs they have shown me. You are so good at drawing, will you take a look?'

'Of course.'

Leela and her mother entered with tea and samosas. 'That's just what I needed. I have been up all night. There was a highway accident, eleven people in the car, all with bones broken. There were lots of unsafe fractures, you know, open wounds. So we were operating all through the night. The senior surgeons went home in the morning, but we had to be there for post-op care.'

He ate hungrily as Munnaji's wife heaped sweet boondis in his plate and spoke to him. 'She is saying the doctor is very good-looking but too thin,' Leela translated for Haruko, giggling.

Prakash spoke about the injuries as he ate. After his third cup of tea, he rose reluctantly. 'I must go. I need to be back at the hospital. I shall come next week.'

'Come as often as you can. It is fun listening to you describing injuries like they are paintings. Besides, Leela loves having you here!'

He left, laughing.

OVER THE NEXT few weeks, Prakash took to dropping by often. He came mostly in the afternoon, either on his way to or from the hospital. He munched on the dry snacks Haruko began keeping in a jar in her room for him, and talked about his work at the hospital – the complicated surgeries he performed, the uncaring senior surgeons who overloaded the resident doctors with work, and the junior doctors who arrived fresh from their college classrooms and knew less than nothing.

'They are not taught anything any longer at the medical college. We knew much more. And they are lazy, one night duty and they will be snoring in the duty room until ten or eleven.'

Once, he came when Haruko was at work. She was setting the last few stones in her project piece. When she finished polishing a setting, she noticed a shadow on the floor and looked up. Prakash stood in the entranceway, watching her.

'I didn't realize you were here! How long have you been waiting?'

'Fifteen minutes or so. You were very focused on your work.' His eyes rested on her in wonder. 'I am like that when I operate. I can't tell who comes in, who goes, who is speaking...'

'I know what you mean. It's like the rest of the world has been cut away, leaving just the bit in your hand at the moment. It is a great feeling, to be entirely there, focused on a single purpose.'

Prakash was unusually quiet and left before Munnaji returned from the gaddi.

'Come tomorrow,' Haruko said as he rose. 'They've been having the annual all-night prayers at the temple for the last couple of nights. Leela has been describing all the delicious food that will come from the temple to every house tomorrow. No one's going to cook, we will all feast on the offerings to the gods!'

'I will see, looks tough,' he replied without turning back.

He did not come the next day, or the day after.

Haruko finished the necklace and paid more attention to teaching Leela and working on the flower ornament. It was turning out first-rate, just as Madanji had said it would. She had mixed pink- and peach-coloured enamels for the petals and a deeper pink for the heart of the iris-jasmine. Diamond dewdrops clustered on the tapered petals, and the pin was shaped like the green stem of a flower.

Prakash came towards the end of the week. He looked fresh and brisk, and declined the tea Leela's sister offered. He checked Haruko's leg. 'How long has it been? Seven weeks?'

'A little over. You had said the cast should come off in eight weeks.'

'We have to see. It was a very bad break. But an X-ray is definitely needed. Nothing can be decided without an X-ray.' He glanced at his watch.

'I will get one done,' Haruko said. 'Maybe you can see it the next time you come or,' she looked directly at him, her long eyes resting on his, 'I can bring it to the hospital. That will save you time.'

Prakash hesitated. 'No, it will be difficult for you. One of my batchmates runs a diagnostic centre not far from here. We can get an X-ray done there right now and I can examine it.'

'Okay. Give me a minute.'

Haruko reached inside the bag lying by her side and, taking a comb, ran it through her dark silken hair. She applied some lip balm.

'I am ready.' She reached for her crutches.

Prakash handed them to her and helped her down the steps. A hot May wind blew strands of her hair across Prakash's face.

'I might as well have not bothered combing them,' Haruko laughed, trying to hold her hair away. 'Sorry, what a mess.' She turned towards the inner rooms and called out, 'I am going for an X-ray. I will be back after the check-up.'

Leela's sisters came to the door and saw them off.

At the clinic, she was wheeled to the X-ray room. 'What is with you and Japan?' she heard the other doctor comment. 'Fiancée in Japan and a Japanese girlfriend here!' The door of the radiology room swung shut and she couldn't hear Prakash's response.

The X-rays were taken quickly and the wet plates were handed to Prakash. He was pleased with what he saw, the serious look disappeared from his eyes.

'You heal quickly,' he said. 'See here and here? The bone is knitting well and the crack in the tibia is hardly visible.'

'So the cast comes off next week?'

'Let's see. We don't want to ruin everything by hurrying, but you can put your weight on this leg now.' He bent and gently eased Haruko's leg to the ground. She swayed for a moment, and clutched at his arm before finding her equilibrium.

On the way back, they crossed the bazaar and Prakash pointed to tall stacks of crisp, honey-coloured discs on display in the sweet shops. 'These are ghevars – sweets for Teej, the rain festival. It is a special festival for women.'

'They look like lacework. So lovely! I'd love to take some for Leela and her sisters.'

Prakash stopped the car before a large shop with a tinted glass front. Inside, people were queuing up before the counters. Women in neatly pinned saris were taking orders and the men behind the counters were weighing and packing.

'Is it crowded because of the festival?' Haruko asked.

'This is the most famous sweet shop in all of Jaipur. It is always crowded in here.'

Prakash placed orders for boxes of ghevar while Haruko waited by one of several circular tables. People were eating, and a delicious smell of food wafted everywhere. He returned with two paper platters. 'Dahi vada. These are made of lentils, a bit like your dumplings. Or are dumplings Chinese?'

The dish was smothered in whipped curd and a dark brown sauce which smelt tangy and spicy. 'Whatever. These smell delicious!' Haruko bit into the soft dumplings and savoured the sweet-and-sour flavours.

'Teej is close,' Prakash said. 'Our dates are around Teej.'

'Dates?'

'Auspicious ones for the wedding. I told you. The first date is in five weeks. It's the best one according to our birth charts.'

'Wow.' Haruko placed her spoon carefully in the paper plate and looked at him. 'That is close. Is she back?'

'Not yet, but her mother and sister are leaving for Japan soon. They will help her pack and all, and she will return with them.'

'Are you looking forward to it?'

'It has been planned for so long and the preparations are almost done,' Prakash stirred the whipped curd. 'And it is the right time now.'

'And you know her very well, I guess. Been together for years, haven't you?'

'Not really. I don't think I know her very well. We went to different schools. She never played with other kids, always running on her own or reading. And she did odd things sometimes. I remember, once she convinced my sister to cut her long hair. I found them in a room, hair strewn everywhere. It was such a shock. She told me that it was to prevent my mother getting headaches. Apparently she had heard my mother say that my sister's long hair gave her such a headache, they required so much care – oiling and washing and careful combing. So she decided on her own to help. She couldn't have been more than six at that time, and she managed to convince my sister who was at least two years older.'

'She seems to have an original way of looking at things. Anyway, what is important is that she is coming back and you are happy.'

Prakash smiled but his eyes had a serious look again.

LEELA'S SCHOOL HOLIDAYS had commenced, and during the whole of the next week, Haruko taught her the basics of metalwork. The baithak took on the appearance of a gaddi, with the two of them hammering and chiselling and soldering metal ornaments. They were both seated on the floor, a metal tray between them, twisting little bits of flat gold sheet into leaf, bird, fish and paisleys shapes. A small heap of the tiny shapes were accumulating on either end of the tray. From time to time, Leela would hold up a piece and then slide it across to Haruko for correction. It was she who saw Prakash and chirruped with joy.

Haruko raised her eyes. 'Hello! What a long time you've been. I thought you'd gone to Japan to bring back the reluctant bride.'

Prakash blushed. 'What Japan? Not everyone can go wherever they please. I have been on emergency duty at the hospital for four days.'

'Gosh. You must be exhausted. Leela, do you think you could make some tea? I don't want your mother to be disturbed.'

Leela placed the forceps in the tray and, carefully shaking her frock over the tray to avoid losing any stray bits of gold which might have fallen in her lap, got up.

'She's already a real sunar,' Haruko said admiringly. 'What have you been up to besides emergency duty?'

'Trying to stay away from the madness at home. Meena will be back next week. Her mother left for Tokyo yesterday with her sister to bring her back.' Prakash extracted a large envelope from his medical bag and held it out to Haruko. 'This is the wedding card. The man at the press called it a mock-up. You remember you said you'd look at it?'

Haruko received the cream-coloured rectangle pasteboard, edged in red and gold, in silence. *Prakash weds Meena* was embossed in gilt lettering on it. She gazed at it for a moment and then took some soft crayons from her leather pencil case. Tacking the card to the back of her sketchbook, she began drawing a vine in its broad margins. The two ends of the vine were held in the curved beaks of a peacock and a peahen. From the vine emerged a sequence of auspicious figures – apsaras, conch shells, fishes, lotus flowers. Leela came in with tea and stood beside Haruko, watching the rich vine take life around the two names on the card. The heat of the late May afternoon baked the street outside, and in the absolute silence, prayer bells from one of the numerous temples in the vicinity could be heard.

About half an hour later, Haruko put her crayons down and turned the card towards Prakash. 'This is one of your ancient Hindu designs. A wishing vine, very auspicious. I saw it in a book my professor gave me. The printer should be able to work from this.'

Prakash looked at the elegant vine curling and flowing around the card. 'It is very beautiful.' He took Haruko's hands in his own, slightly sweaty ones. 'I don't know how to thank you.'

'You just did.' Haruko leaned over and kissed him. 'Congratulations, Prakash.'

She felt his hesitant hand rest on her back for a moment. 'I will bring Meena over next week,' he said before leaving.

That night, Leela lingered in Haruko's room, leafing through her books as Haruko sat in silence, her eyes abstracted. 'Jiji, what is this?' she asked, pointing at the picture of a terracotta-coloured bowl, deep and shaped like a cupped palm. The bowl had uneven golden lines running all over it.

Haruko glanced at the picture. 'That's a broken clay bowl mended with gold.' Leela's eyes widened. 'Isn't it beautiful? I had tried my hand at the art of kintsugi in a ceramic class one semester.'

Leela looked at the picture again. The bowl did have a curious beauty, independent of its shape, colour, the trailing golden seams. But being a goldsmith's daughter, mending clay with precious gold seemed sacrilegious to her. 'It seems wastage, Jiji. Can it hold water?'

'Not all vessels are meant to hold water, some are for allowing water to seep away.' Haruko trailed a finger over the photograph. 'Broken things are precious too.'

There was a brief silence. 'Do you want I sleep here tonight, Jiji?' Leela asked softly.

Haruko looked at the dark eyes fixed on her with earnestness and shook her head. 'No, I am okay. But I can show you a cool way of braiding your hair before you go to bed.'

Leela fetched a comb and some hairbands, and sat on the floor with her back towards Haruko who loosened her long plait and began weaving her hair, strand over strand, in a palm-leaf pattern.

A FEW NIGHTS later, the first rains fell. Haruko woke up and, amid the sound of rain in the street, heard a knock on her door. The knock, like a palm striking the wooden door, was repeated.

'Who's there?' she called.

'It's me.'

Haruko got up quickly and, not bothering with the crutches, limped to the door. She opened it to let Prakash in.

He stepped in, his shoes leaving wet mud marks on the floor. Haruko closed the door quietly and switched on her solar lamp. Prakash's clothes were damp and wrinkled, his cheeks stubbly like he was returning from round-the-clock duty at the hospital. He did not have his glasses on and blinked in the light of the lamp, his lashes wet. Haruko could not bear to look at his naked eyes. She took his hand and led him to the bed and put her arm around his shoulders.

'What happened, Prakash?' He let his head fall on to her shoulder. His sobs shook her. She felt his tears through her thin cotton T-shirt. 'Hush, what's the matter? What happened?'

Unable to speak, he sank into her helplessly, his body collapsing heavily against her. She held him in her arms, drawing his head to her bosom. 'Hush, hush, it can't be that bad.' She rocked him gently. His words were inaudible against her breasts, fluttering across her skin in sharp breaths and sobs. There was no need for him to say anything, she knew what it was, what it must be. Only partings could cause such tearing, incomprehensible grief.

She bent and kissed the vein trembling in Prakash's temple and ran her palm down his back, pressing him closer.

He raised his head. 'Meena is not coming back, ever ... Not for me. She doesn't want to...'

'You will have to bear it, Prakash. It is perhaps better this way, not returning is better than coming back and then leaving.' She touched his damp cheeks with her fingertips.

'It is better, you'll be happy yet. She will fade like something imaginary, something made of light and shade.'

He looked at Haruko with his unbearable hurt eyes. 'How is it possible? How could she do this to us, lie to all of us?'

'Don't think like that, Prakash. Perhaps she didn't lie, perhaps she just forgot. We have these blind spots, all of us. Sometimes we run across one and forget everything for a while...'

Prakash shook his head. 'You don't understand, she won't return, Haruko. Not for me, never. She hasn't forgotten, she remembers very well that wedding preparations are being made, invitations have been sent to everyone ... Relatives, friends, they all know ... She remembered all this time, while she was telling us her lies – I will be back soon, I am working hard to complete the thesis, it won't be long now, fix the date after winter, after spring, this summer ... And all the while she knew she wasn't coming back ... She remembered all through...'

Haruko cradled him against her and lightly kissed his eyes, his cheeks, his mouth. 'You'll be okay, you'll be okay.'

His breath swelled and his arms holding her body tightened, he pulled her closer, his mouth crushed hers. He tugged at her T-shirt, his hands seeking her breasts, squeezing them until she winced. He pushed her down on the bed and, pulling off his trousers, straddled her. His surgeon's fingers slipped and fumbled as he tried to enter her. Haruko shifted her injured leg out of the way and guided him. He pushed inside her with his full weight. Strange moans escaped through his gritted teeth and sweat poured from his body, until finally he collapsed on her.

They lay entangled until the glass ventilators set high up in the wall turned from dark velvet to dirty grey and birds began calling. Prakash rose and pulled on his damp clothes. Opening the door softly, he stepped out into the street. He did not say anything, did not turn to look back. Haruko watched him go in silence.

When Leela came later in the morning with Haruko's breakfast, she saw the muddy footmarks on the floor. Haruko, her face averted, was scrubbing her cast, cleaning the mud from it. Fetching a mop, Leela cleaned the floor and quietly took the damp and stained bedcover away for washing.

OVER THE NEXT few days, Haruko worked all day, completing the assignments Madanji had given her. She told him she planned to leave by the end of the week, and did not take new work on. As she worked, Leela noticed the air of waiting around her, and the way she raised her head to glance at the door at the slightest sound. The day after she handed the last finished ornament to Madanji, she went to the hospital with Leela.

It was early afternoon, and the OPD was crowded. A junior doctor looked at Haruko's X-ray, made her lie on a hard, steel bed, and sliced the plaster off her leg with a small, circular, electrical saw which slipped and bit into her leg. She walked out of the hospital, her leg free of the dragging cast, holding Leela's hand for balance. They took an auto rickshaw back to the lane in the old city. The bazaar was crowded with women in festive clothing, and there were buntings and tinsel strung on shopfronts.

'I have booked my ticket for Bombay, I'll leave tomorrow,' she told Leela when they reached home. Leela cried quietly. Haruko put an arm around her and they sat silent, side by side, on the threshold of the baithak.

Later that day, Haruko sorted her belongings and finished packing. Then she went out into the lanes to thank Madanji and his artisans. In the evening, she set tasks for Leela to complete over the remaining month of her school holidays. 'This should keep you busy for weeks, and when you are finished with it, look around and you will find much to learn. These guys, your father, your uncles, they are phenomenal. I have learnt so much from them. You can learn too, if you really wish, if you keep at it. Just observe and you'll absorb, my professor used to say.' She held out the little velvet box containing the hair ornament towards Leela. 'One day, you might make another one like this and complete the pair. If you do, write to me at my email address, it will always find me. If not, that's okay too. Just think of this as your wedding gift from me.'

Leela accepted the box, holding it in her cupped hands, her eyes brimming with tears. Haruko hugged her briefly.

The next day, she left for Bombay.

MEENA

THE ROAD LEFT the last suburbs of Tokyo behind, and the slopes and summits of Hakone's gently rising hills came into view.

Yuri turned to me. 'The mountains are magnificent, Meenu-chan, you shall enjoy them very much.' Her careful English and slow cadence were full of charm to me. Only very infrequently would she slip and an 'r' would turn into an 'l', but that was charming too, like a child's lisping.

Mountains evoked memories for me, they were part of my childhood. Almost every summer, as I was growing up, my parents bravely packed suitcases and holdalls, filled tiffin boxes with food cooked early in the morning, and set off on slow, meandering train journeys to the mountains with the three of us, my two sisters and I, in tow. Shimla, Nainital, Ooty, Darjeeling. My summer vacations were spent following crowds around lakes and quaint hill-station bazaars, eating sticky peanut sweets and spicy savouries. One of my earliest childhood memories is of one such holiday: We are walking by a green lake gleaming in the soft mountain sunlight, my elder sister and I. I am holding tightly on to her hand, afraid of the iron hooves of horses trotting all around us. There is a distinctive odour in the air, an odour composed of sweat and dung. To me, horses were as much a feature of our mountain holidays as the scenic mall roads and lovers' points, and the smell of horse dung is inextricably connected with mountains in my memory. Involuntarily, I tried to detect it in the fresh, pine-and-cedar scented air of Hakone. But of course there were no horses here. The smooth, concrete-and-metal road running through the gently rising and falling hills had sparse traffic, a few cars, an occasional limousine bus, like the one Yuri and I were riding.

The mountains were mesmerizing in their summer beauty, even on an overcast day like today when the sky was curdled with dense white clouds and the daylight falling on the green trees was muted and grey. The meadows by the roadside were dotted with white daisies and yellow primroses. Little lanes, overhung with trees and full of a mysterious grey-green light, ran up and down the hills.

'This is too beautiful to catch a glimpse of from the bus window, Yuri. Can't we just get down here and walk to the hotel? It can't be very far now, and the slope's gentle.' In the quiet bus, my voice rang out despite my effort to speak in a soft, low tone. The middle child of three and growing up in a noisy, extended family, I had learnt early to drown out other voices in order to be heard, and a few months in Japan under Yuri's tutelage had not had much effect.

Yuri shook her head. 'The bus has scheduled stops. We must wait for our stop.'

'Come on, Yuri. Surely we can ask the driver very, very politely to make an unscheduled one? I'm sure he won't mind. Back home, we do it all the time! Let's, please. He would only need to stop the bus for a few seconds. The man controls the machine, isn't it?'

Yuri smiled, but shook her head firmly. 'I am very sorry but we cannot do that. It would be impolite to place the driver in such difficulty. He would have to choose between refusing a request and breaking a rule.'

I gave in. I knew that despite the gentle tone, those were strong words from Yuri.

I HAD MET Yuri at a language exchange class organized by the advisor for international students at the University of Tokyo. I had come to Tokyo on a research scholarship, and Yuri was studying political economy. We were paired up for the evening, me to practise my halting, beginner's Japanese, and Yuri to practise her fairly good English. I had mentioned to her that I was researching woman-themed Japanese literature for my project. She had smiled politely and made the appropriate remarks. As the evening progressed, I found myself telling her all about my dislocated life in Tokyo. The beautiful university campus filled largely with Japanese students was like a world sealed away behind a glass wall to me – I could never be part of it. I was living on campus at that time, and shared my room with another visiting student, a Slovenian who belonged to a tight circle of East European students in Tokyo. She was out with them every evening, and I spent my evenings alone, eating dry cereal and watching Japanese television with subtitles to improve my language proficiency. I was vegetarian and, with my limited knowledge of the Japanese script, was unable to decipher the ingredients listed on boxes of food articles in a jumble of kanji, katakana and hiragana. Yuri was astonished and dismayed to hear that I had been surviving on cereal, yoghurt and fruits all this while. 'I am sorry you have so much trouble in Japan, so sorry you face difficulties in my country.' She had bowed deeply. 'You need much looking after,' she had said, not critically but sympathetically. From that evening onwards, she had become my guide in Tokyo.

Yuri worked part-time at a Japanese magazine's offices, reviewing drafts and reading proofs, to pay her tuition, and lived in a tiny apartment in nearby Kasuga not far from the subway station. After her classes, she took to dropping by at my room on the campus. She would sit unobtrusively in a corner while I worked, quietly turning the pages of books I had brought with me from home – the Ramayana, Phanishwarnath Renu's novels, Agyeya's poetry. The Devanagari script in which the Sanskrit and Hindi texts were written was like so many squiggles and symbols to her, and yet she could remain engrossed, occasionally casting glances at me as I looked up references and typed my notes. When my day's quota of work was done, Yuri would take me to explore Tokyo – downtown Ginza, Harajuku, Shibuya, Omotesando, suburban Ueno.

One weekend, we rode the Marunouchi and Hanzomon lines to the Sanja-sama shrine in Asakusa district. The stone torii gate of the temple and its façade, painted a vivid vermillion in the Shinto tradition and glowing like a beacon in the noonday sun, was visible as soon as we turned into the historic district. The narrow streets leading to the temple were lined on both sides with shops selling sweets and souvenirs. Crowds of tourists and devotees milled around and the smell of incense wafted everywhere. To me, the whole effect was not unlike an Indian temple town, only cleaner and far more orderly. The temple compound was large and, despite the crowds, a place of peace. I followed Yuri's lead and poured water from a long-stemmed wooden ladle over my hands. We stood before the idol-less sanctum in silence, our heads bowed. Candles flickered in the dim interior. The high altar was flanked by vases filled with chrysanthemums, and the bells hanging from the ceiling at the entrance were muffled with red cloth looped into graceful folds. The only sounds were those of coins dropping into the wooden offering box and people softly clapping their hands twice as they bent from the waist in obeisance.

After praying, we explored the temple compound. Wooden prayer tablets inscribed with supplications for good luck and paper scrolls hung from shade trees as young, soft-faced Shinto maidens sold fortunes and charms from small shops located around the courtyard. I watched them with fascination. They were dressed in white and vermillion blouses and loose trousers, their hair parted neatly in the middle and a spray of blue hydrangea flowers pinned to their foreheads. They seemed ethereal to me, their every action, every movement gentle and peaceful like a prayer. Yuri bought me a charm, a tiny pouch made of exquisite white brocaded silk.

'It is for academic success,' she said. 'Especially meant for students, Meenu-chan.'

We emerged from the temple complex into the crowded streets. Yuri had made a booking at a nearby restaurant for our lunch and we walked towards it. Up ahead, the tall tower of Tokyo Skytree glittered with coloured electric lights despite the bright afternoon. It faced the torii gate of the temple – its antithesis in every way.

I turned to Yuri. 'Which one of these is the real Tokyo, Yuri?'

'Both are, Meenu-chan. Tokyo is a city of past and future, living in the present. Just like us, we, with our bits of past and future, try to live in the present too.'

'How beautifully you put it. You should write waka poetry.'

'I try to,' she replied quietly and, holding my elbow, gently steered me to the left.

'I didn't know you wrote poetry. You've never mentioned it earlier!'

'Haven't I?' She smiled her quiet smile. 'But we must hurry, our table is booked for one p.m. The tofu restaurant is as famous for its punctuality as it is for its food. If we are not there on time, they will give the table to others.'

I was not surprised that Yuri had never spoken about writing poetry. It was typical of her. She held herself under a rigid discipline of politeness, always willing to listen to others, speaking sparingly about herself, and that too upon my asking. She had told me she was an only child and had left the old town of Nara after high school, where her parents ran a traditional ryokan, a Japanese-style guest house, from their home. I was curious about Nara – its tiered pagodas and famous shrines, the great bronze Buddha of Todai-ji and the holy deer roaming its streets, reverently fed by visitors – and had wondered what it was like to grow up in the ancient capital of Japan. Yuri had answered my questions factually, in her usual gentle way. Yes, the Vairochana Buddha was beautiful. The shrines were generally crowded, especially around festival days and the ryokan was always full. The deer were very forward – they snatched food from the hands of devotees, kicking them with their sharp hooves if annoyed, and they smelled. I could sense some reluctance in Yuri's replies. She mentioned her parents fleetingly, did not mention any friends or relatives. Her solitariness surprised me. Her acceptance of it as a natural condition of being, even more so.

MY CROWDED LIFE couldn't have been more different from Yuri's minimalistic one. My parents and two sisters, my numerous uncles, aunts and cousins, who all took an intrusive, voluble interest in my life, quickly became known to Yuri. My parents Skyped with me frequently to check on me. *Are you studying hard?* they would ask. *Don't waste your time, you have to complete the thesis and return. The neighbour's son is already in the second year of his MS, soon he'll be a big doctor, he won't wait forever,* they reminded me on every call. My two sisters Skyped with me too, and were disappointed that I was doing just what my parents expected and spending my time on completing my project, that I had no one more interesting to show them than demure Yuri. Uncles, aunts and distant relations called as well to confirm that I was indeed at a university in Japan and had not eloped with someone unsuitable.

The neighbour's son, Prakash, that eternal refrain in my parents' conversation, called occasionally. My sisters and I and Prakash and his sisters had grown up together. There was an understanding between his parents and mine. I remember Prakash's mother stroking my hair, my cheek, and saying, *She is ours,* and my mother, glowing with pride, nodding. My desirability as a daughter-in-law was an endorsement of her skill in bringing me up. *Girls are like clay,* she was fond of saying, *I have kept mine soft, you can mould them as you like.* I resented it, resented being compared to a pat of shapeless clay, to be pounded and pulled and pinched into shape. Some of that resentment fastened on to Prakash. I did wild things to annoy him, spilled paint on his cricket whites, punctured his bicycle. Once, I stole his science notebook right before an exam and watched him search anxiously for it all day. In the end, I returned it to him. It was so painstakingly illustrated with diagrams of the frogs and rats Prakash had dissected that I couldn't bear to throw it in the empty lot behind our houses as I had planned. He took it in silence and didn't tell on me – my sister did. She saw me handing the notebook to Prakash and tattled to my mother. I was not allowed to step out of the house for days and all my favourite books were confiscated, but it didn't matter. Now when he called and asked his stock questions, I couldn't tell him how I dreaded them, how they bored me with their repetitiveness. *How's the weather there? Are you eating well? Anything new and fresh?* he'd ask, and I'd answer as best I could. To keep the awkward silence we were always in danger of lapsing into at bay, I chattered about Yuri, Tokyo, my work.

My parents liked Yuri very much, her gentle calm carried over even low-resolution Skype. *She is a good influence,* my mother took to saying, *always soft-spoken, always polite. See how still she sits, how softly she speaks? You should learn from her. You make my head swim the way you walk about while talking.* If I told her that Yuri had taken me to nightclubs and bars in Tokyo, that I had begun eating fish and meat under her tutelage, her approval would have quickly changed to angry shock. For, to my mother, these were cardinal sins, dishonouring the upbringing she had given me. She proudly recounted to everyone that, as a child, I had recoiled in horror when offered chicken wings at a party. *I don't eat birds,* I had apparently said in my loud voice. That story had always annoyed me. I felt forever trapped in the opinions of a three-year-old. When, at a popular sushi bar in Ginza, Yuri had said with a suggestive smile on her lips, 'Try, please, Meenu-chan. Forbidden can be pleasurable,' I had accepted without much persuasion, had tasted the tuna sushi and California rolls, and had enjoyed their unfamiliar flavours. My turning non-vegetarian had made our outings easier to plan. We were able to eat anywhere, instead of worrying about where to find vegetarian food half the time and hunting for vegetarian restaurants the rest.

It had made the decision to take a trip into the mountains simpler too. Yuri had suggested we spend a weekend in Hakone. 'It is more scenic than Nikko, much more secluded, and yet close enough to Tokyo,' she had said. 'And the hot springs are an experience.' I had told my parents about the three-hour bus journey and the plan to spend a couple of nights in Hakone. They had fretted about the cold in the mountains though it was May, and had asked me to pack sufficient dry food in case there wasn't proper food available. *And be careful about American soldiers,* my mother had told me again and again. My younger sister had introduced my mother to *Japan Times* online, setting it as the default website on the computer at home. My mother had taken to reading it every day, laboriously deciphering the English words to find out about weather and crime in Japan. She had read about the murder of a young Japanese girl by an American soldier from a US military base, one of the few crimes to occur in Japan, and it had become a recurring theme with her. I mailed her news stories about Japan's low crime rate and safety record with respect to women, but my assurances had no effect. She continued to fear dangers, named and nameless, lurking everywhere. What I did not tell her was that I walked everywhere – inside the campus, to the supermarket outside the university, through Roppongi at night – wearing anything I wanted, a miniskirt or a pair of shorts or my long kurta, and no one stared or whistled or tried to paw me. Telling her would have been of no use – she would have missed the point. In fact, she would have been angry. *Where are your brains?* she would have scolded me. *Why would you invite trouble in a foreign land by dressing like a loose woman? And what would Prakash think if he came to know?* I, too, wondered what he would think. What if he saw Yuri and me in one of the Ginza bars, in barely-there mini-dresses, Yuri drinking beer, me sipping a lemon soda, couples all around us leaning into each other, kissing intimately? Would it light a match in his nerves, make his blood flow quicker? But then I remembered the hospital smell of disinfectants that clung to him, his dry, clean hands, his stock phrases. I knew he would not approve.

'WE ARE IN luck Meenu-chan,' Yuri spoke, her voice hushed. 'There is Mount Fuji. Rare it is to see Fuji-san so clearly, without clouds. People wait for days for such a perfect sighting.'

I gazed at the perfect, gently sloping cone of Fuji, blue and white with distance and snow, rising behind the rolling green hills in the foreground.

'Rather like an icy, arrogant beauty, Fuji-san is, no Yuri?'

Yuri clapped her hands softly in approval, 'There is a haiku in there, Meenu-chan. The icy, arrogant beauty, omnipresent, unattainable, disdaining my touch.'

'You're a poet, Yuri. What you are doing among the dry dregs of political economy, only you know!'

Yuri's eyes shone, but her mouth resumed its demure lines.

The hotel Yuri had chosen was in the Japanese style, with paper-covered shoji doors and two futon beds, placed side by side on the tatami floor-mats.

Yuri apologized profusely. 'How thoughtless of me, Meenu-chan. Sleeping on the floor would be inconvenient for you.'

'Come on, Yuri. What inconvenience? This is all so quaint and pretty! I'd love to take that scroll in the alcove, the one with Japanese black pines painted on it, back to Tokyo to hang beside my desk. It would bring the mountains to my room. Also that head of hydrangea in the vase next to it!'

'You can't take the scroll, it is hotel property, Meenu-chan. But the hydrangea you may. We'd need to inform housekeeping that you are removing the flowers though.'

'I was kidding, Yuri!' I said.

Yuri smiled softly. 'We should eat lunch now, Meenu-chan. It is already late. Would you like to go to one of the nice restaurants in Sankyo-Mae or Hakone-machi?'

We drank a quick cup of Japanese tea. Yuri tied up her hair, and I put on a cardigan over my sweatshirt. I had bought it at a discount store in Tokyo at my mother's insistence. *The weather in the mountains is always changing,* she had said, fretting. *Japan Times says minimum temperature of sixteen degrees in Hakone this weekend. If you catch a cold, who will look after you over there? Plus you would lose study time.*

Out in the open, the mountain air was indeed chilly, and I was grateful for my cardigan. Yuri shivered delicately. She was dressed in a soft, full-sleeved cotton top tucked into the waist of dainty cotton trousers, and wore pumps with lace socks, her clothes more suitable for a walk in fashionable Shibuya rather than along a mountain road.

'You must be cold, Yuri,' I said. 'My mother had mentioned the low temperatures these few days. But I just thought she was fussing as usual...'

'Don't worry, the walk will warm us up.' She reached out and took my arm. 'You feel nice and warm.'

We walked briskly, and I soon felt warm enough to take my cardigan off. The road climbed through the meadows and pine forests we had seen from the bus, and every once in a while we broke from our path to follow a shaded wild lane and see where it led. It was late afternoon by the time we reached the small town of Hakone-machi and decided to eat at a Japanese restaurant on the main street. It had sprays of daisies and wild grass in the windows, and the light inside was warm and mild. We sat with our bare feet tucked under us, and the owner and his wife served. They brought us bowls of soba noodles with dashi, hot tempura and summer greens, and bitter-clean-tasting Japanese tea. The food was excellent and we thanked them profusely. After lunch, we walked under the tall pines along Lake Ashi. The trees were ancient, their immense, moss-covered trunks rose skyward like massive pillars. Across the road were a few cafés and, in the distance, we could see a shrine. Soon, the wind picked up and the lake was full of curled waves. It became cold enough to numb our faces.

'Should we head back to our hotel, Yuri?' I still worried about her flimsy clothes.

'Yes, but suppose we go in there first?' Yuri pointed to a small bar across from the lake. A stone jar filled with water plants and small, darting fish was placed outside its door, and a bamboo cage with chirping crickets hung from the wooden roof above.

'It's so quaint!' I exclaimed.

Yuri nodded. 'The owner has a taste for old beauty.'

We entered the low-roofed bar and were served saké in beautiful grey-green clay cups, small enough to be held in the hollow of my palm. I had never tasted alcohol before.

'It is cold, Meenu-chan, and in Japan, a mountain evening and saké are considered a perfect combination. You have tried one, now you must try the other.'

Yuri held the cup out to me. I sipped the rice beverage slowly, running my fingers along the rough surface of the saké cup, and regarded Yuri sitting across from me. She had tossed down her saké and was pouring herself another cupful. Her eyes glistened as she looked up at me, and her rosy mouth relaxed.

'It is not strong, Meenu-chan, don't worry.' She smiled. 'Drink up. It is impolite to not match your companion cup for cup!' she said, and filled my half-empty one.

As we drank cup after cup of the saké, her cheeks became flushed. I too felt an unaccustomed warmth inside me, spreading in pleasant waves to the core of my body. It was dark by the time we stepped out.

'I compliment you on your drinking, Meenu-chan. You hold the saké well. It has only made your lovely eyes brighter.'

I laughed, savouring the warmth inside as the cold air played on my face. The night, fragrant with multitudinous scents layered one over another, held the mountains in its shadowy arms and there was an intimate silence, unbroken save for an occasional car or a late crow's petulant cry. Yuri gently took my hand in her own as we walked side by side.

BACK AT THE hotel, she took out yukatas from the cloth cases laid out neatly on our futons.

'This is a day of new sensations. You must try the onsen now, Meenu-chan,' she handed a yukata, blue with sprigs of white cherry blossoms printed across it, to me. 'You wear it gathered on the left and tied with the cloth belt.'

I held up the cotton garment. It had long, very wide sleeves, rather like the housecoat that my mother sometimes wore at home and which all of us hated. I stepped into the small en suite bathroom and, quickly taking off my jeans and sweatshirt, slipped into the yukata, winding the cloth belt tightly around my waist. I gathered my loose hair into a bun and speared them into place with a long wooden pin. When I emerged, Yuri was dressed and ready too, hair tied at the nape of her neck, small feet in shiny geta slippers.

'You look like a classical Japanese print, Yuri-chan!' I said, smiling.

'And you like one of those anime characters with huge eyes and a tiny waist! This blue is the right colour for you.'

The onsen was a large bathing area with changing rooms, shower stalls, indoor and outdoor pools filled with hot, mineral-rich water from the mountain spring. It was empty of people at this time, save for a lone old Japanese lady in one corner of the indoor hot pool with a small moist towel draped on her head. In the changing room, Yuri removed her Yukata and stepped into a bathing stall. She wore nothing underneath. She stepped into a bathing stall and sat on a low plastic stool, rubbing herself vigorously with a washcloth. I looked through my lashes at her pale, straight back and narrow hips. Water from the overhead shower fell on her in shining rivulets. Averting my eyes, I undressed with clumsy haste and showered hurriedly, draping the towel around me once I was done. Yuri finished drying herself and, dropping her towel in a bamboo basket, called quietly to me.

'Meenu-chan, the outdoor hot pool is very pleasurable in the evening. Come.'

She slid the glass door dividing the indoor bathing area from the outdoor one and walked out, naked. I could see her skin prickling at the touch of the cold air. I had bathed in hot springs and rivers before, with my mother, sisters, female cousins and aunts, but never like this. Everyone was always fully clothed, the older women in saris and the younger ones in salwar kameez or slacks and long tops.

Yuri looked at me and laughed. 'You bathe in a towel, Meenu-chan? Earth has stirred her minerals in the mountain spring for you to soak in, not this towel!'

I blushed and, dropping my towel, entered the shallow lava-stone pool and sat cross-legged on the rock floor, the water reaching up to my breasts. The water was bubbling hot and felt silken on my limbs, tired and drowsy from the long walk and the alcohol. There were green trees all around the pool, their leaves glossy and gleaming with night-dew under the yellow electric lights. Outside the bright arc cast by the lights, the clear mountain night had settled like a transparent, dark veil.

'Look at the mountains, Meenu-chan. They look close at hand, but they are beyond reach, aren't they?' Yuri turned her glistening eyes towards me.

'Mountains are special to you, Yuri? I have never seen you so animated.'

'My mother was from Hakone, from these mountains.'

'Now I see! When did she move to Nara?'

'The one in Nara is my stepmother. I lived in Hakone as a child.'

'Wow. The things I don't know about you!'

Yuri smiled a half smile, her cheeks were flushed. 'My real mother used to say that mountains are like beautiful strangers – you desire them but cannot know them.' She scooped up water in her cupped hand and watched it drip in glistening drops from her fingers. 'She used to take me up and down the mountain roads on her bicycle, in a little basket seat, singing songs about their timeless beauty. She'd stop at quiet corners, lift me over wooden fences, run in the meadows with me, pick daisies and wild flowers, dance in the grass. She'd hold me close and kiss me...'

The pool now felt uncomfortably hot, and my blood beat in my veins, pulsating behind my ears and above my navel from the heat. I rose on my sluggish legs and sat on the cold rocks beside the pool, hugging my knees to my chest. Yuri too stepped out and sat on the opposite side, leaning back, her palms on the rocks on either side of her slim body, her legs stretched out.

'You love her very much, Yuri-chan?'

'Yes. She too loved me very much, but not enough. Not so much as she loved someone else.' She paused and then added, 'Another man, a man not my father. I was five when she met a man, a foreigner. He dressed smarter than my father. I remember, he had beautiful hands, and when he kissed my mother, I could see her tremble as she never did when I kissed her.'

I looked sideways at her. She was golden and supple as she lay against the beige lava rocks, like the pale bamboo I had glimpsed in the mountains of Hakone. My eyes slid along her long waist, her flat belly, her pale translucent feet, her small breasts rising with her breath which misted over her.

'Perhaps it was not love, Yuri, just desire. It would pass. Perhaps she didn't realize how it affected you. I hope you don't hold it against her.'

'I was only six, Meenu-chan. Wisdom was far away, pain very near.' Yuri's voice had become softer still, and I strained my ears to hear her. 'You who have a mother and father and sisters and many, many more, could you see into the heart of a six-year-old losing the only person who gave her joyful love?' Yuri crossed over to my side of the pool and sat facing me. The exquisite mountain breeze, laden with green fragrances, fanned our heated bodies. 'I am of another world, Meenu-chan, a world that's not real to you, isn't it? My mother, a poet in love with the mountains, married my father, a shopkeeper by trade. Why did she? I could not understand, still cannot.' I took Yuri's hand in mine and pressed it. Yuri moved closer. 'My father owned a convenience store and a teashop. He never had time for poetry or for a small girl who could not wipe a cup without breaking it. Only my mother, only she brought beauty and love in my life. Do you see what her loving another man more meant to me?' Yuri's eyes were bright, but the tears in them refused to fall. 'We no longer ran together in the meadows. She began sending me out to play by myself. Some days, I stole back, peeped through the windows, and saw my mother's cherry-blossom body naked in bed, the man like a pale ugly slug clinging to her. Yet she was crazy about him...'

Yuri fell silent. It was getting colder. We stepped back into the steaming pool. The lava rocks at the base of the pool felt warm and coarse, and vapour rose from our bodies as the steaming water washed over our cold skins. .

'I wish you could see what I saw, as I saw, Meenu-chan...'

'Perhaps I can't see, Yuri. A six-year-old could not have understood, but you are not six any longer, now you can understand. Your mother just happened to fall in love with a stranger with beautiful hands. But that love could not have replaced the love she had for you.'

Yuri lowered her head. The yellow electric lights and rising steam enveloped her in a shining mist. She cried soundlessly, her mouth closed, her face rigid. I wiped her tears and gently stroked her hair. They felt sleek and heavy with water under my dripping fingers. Yuri reached out her slim arms and drew me to her. She rested her head against my shoulder. Her breath felt like warm fingers on my neck. Her lips moved, but no sound came from them. A light misty rain, like an icy twin of the steam rising from the hot pool, began falling. I could feel the spasms running through Yuri's body as she held on to me, her breasts resting against me as her breath came and went.

'What happened eventually, Yuri? What did your mother do?'

Yuri raised her head, her tears had stopped. 'That man didn't really want her, he never loved her like I did. He just wanted to sleep with her occasionally, and for that he destroyed everything. She left me ... There was no one left for me to love...'

'Where did she go?'

'She is still here,' Yuri said softly. 'One afternoon, she was fetching me from the nursery. A car came from the opposite side, very fast. It passed very close to my mother's bicycle. I felt the rush of wind against my face and ducked in my basket seat. My mother lost her balance and fell. I was thrown into the roadside hedges, and she fell in the middle of the road.

I was not allowed to see her ... her beautiful body mauled by another oncoming car. My father sent me to stay with my aunt in Kobe for a while, a long while. In the end, he sold his shop here, left the mountains forever and settled in Nara. I never saw her again, Meenu-chan. My mother ... the woman I loved...'

Yuri's right hand fluttered on my thigh, her left palm was under my right breast, her thumb caressed its swell right up to the nipple. I felt waves rise from a subterranean place in me, swirl, rush like a hot spring. I pressed my buttocks against the rough stone floor.

'Here I am in the mountains again with a beautiful woman I love,' Yuri whispered in my ear. 'I think my mother sees me, feels what I had felt and also that which I will never feel...'

LEELA

LEELA PULLED THE accordion-like wooden doors together and locked the gaddi. The blue paint on the doors was peeling away in long, curling strips. It was evening. Overhead, the grey sky was streaked with peach and pink. Leela looked at the colours swelling in wave- and feather-like formations and nodded. *Yes, indeed, they are possible, all colours are possible.* The air in the alley smelt of evening meals being prepared. She was late. With both her sisters now married, she knew her mother needed her help in the kitchen and hurried home. The haveli's once pink façade was bleached to a faint flush. It hadn't been painted these few years, and dark streaks, traces of rain and accumulated dirt, were visible all over.

Leela walked through the open gate. Last year, one of the hinges of the gate had given and it dragged on the cracked stone flags below. Her mother let it stand open all day, closing it only at night. Munnaji liked it open, it allowed him to glimpse the goings-on in the street from where he lay in the baithak, a street he used to walk down several times during the day until a few years ago.

Leela washed her hands and feet at the tap in the inner courtyard and, shaking the drops of water off, entered the kitchen. The single bulb cast its light on the gas stove on which the pressure cooker whistled, steam building inside it. Her mother was kneading dough. The rest of the kitchen was immersed in diaphanous shadows.

'Late as always. You know the gaddi must be at rest when day and night come together, no one should touch their tools of trade when the two times meet.' Her mother pushed a basket of green beans towards Leela.

'Madan Kako-sa has promised to deliver a pair of kangans to his client by the end of this week. I had to complete one today,' Leela said and began chopping the beans. 'Such poor quality enamel work it had. Pappaji would not have touched it, but Madan Kako-sa is always in hurry. *Quickly, quickly, let's do shortcut,* he keeps saying. He only used to listen to Pappaji.'

'Once your Pappaji is better, he will ensure only good work comes to our gaddi. There is no kundansaaz like him.'

'That's true. But I have become quite good at setting the polki too, the artisans in the bazaar say so. Only Kako-sa gives me such poor pieces to work on ... If I could work on the pieces Pappaji used to, I think I could be as good.'

'You have a long tongue, Leela. Hurry up with the beans. It's time for your Pappaji's dinner. We can't eat polki and kundan.'

'I can survive on that...' Leela muttered and reached for a pan to cook the beans in.

When the food was ready, Leela's mother set aside the first two rotis for a cow and a dog and smeared the third with ghee and sugar. She placed it in a worn silver dish and carried it over to the shrine in a corner of the kitchen, and rang a small silver bell to alert the gods of the offering. Leela rolled out balls of fresh dough and cooked more rotis. When her mother finished her prayers, Leela served her father's dinner in a large steel platter, sweetening a small bowl of curd with crumbled jaggery for him.

'You feed Pappaji. I will make rotis for the upstairs folk,' she said to her mother.

The 'upstairs folk' were two young men – cousins, who both worked as representatives for a pharmaceuticals company and had rented the rooms on the first floor of the haveli. They depended on Leela's mother's kitchen for their meals and paid for the food along with their monthly rent. Taking money for their food embarrassed her mother. 'When your Pappaji was well, I would not let anyone who stepped over the threshold go without food, and now I have to take money from these boys who are so far away from their families, their mothers...'

Almost the entire haveli was now rented out. The ground floor to a family who worked in the savoury shops and the second floor to an old craftsman. Leela's mother bemoaned the fact that the haveli built by their ancestors for the family now housed strangers. But it could not be helped, the rent kept the household running.

'Take their food upstairs, but tell them if they don't come to the kitchen to get it next time, they can sleep hungry. We can't be ferrying their food as if they were sons of kings.' Leela filled a steel tiffin carrier with food for the two. She slipped in some lime and green chilli pickle, a small smile forming at the corners of her mouth. She knew Manish enjoyed its tangy, hot flavour with his food. 'It is hardly appropriate for a girl from a respectable family to mingle with strange men,' her mother continued grumbling as Leela closed the tiffin carrier.

HER MOTHER HAD said similar things when Leela had first started working at Madanji's gaddi, and again when she had reopened their own gaddi after a hiatus of almost four years. It had remained closed ever since the accident that had left Munnaji with a broken spine and a broken spirit.

The accident had happened one early summer morning. Munnaji had left home for the fruit market, riding pillion on their neighbour's son's bike. The first crop of mangoes had arrived earlier that week, and it was time to make the annual offering of mangoes at the family shrine so that everyone could feast on the king of fruits. The boy had lost control of the bike when an elephant had suddenly come into view around a bend in the road. The bike had skidded and overturned. The neighbour's son had died on the spot and Munnaji had lain on the road screaming in agony while the elephant stood by, calmly munching on the hay it carried in its trunk. Eventually, the elephant's mahout was able to fetch help and take the dead and the wounded to the hospital. Leela considered it a mercy that the accident had slipped out of her father's memory, like so many other things.

While her father lay broken in the hospital, her mother was inconsolable and the houses up and down the street filled with wailing in sympathy. Leela sorely missed Dadi-sa. She would have known how to calm her mother, what to cook for her father, which gods to propitiate. But Dadi-sa had died a year before the accident, not long after Haruko had left. Leela remembered the day she had left for heaven clearly. It had begun well – a parcel had arrived for her bearing a Bombay postmark, the first ever parcel with her name on it. It was from Haruko and contained a set of drawing implements, a book on the history of European fine jewellery, and prints of the ornaments Haruko had made. There was a note too, unsigned: *Trust you are continuing with your learning. Your father is a real artist, learn by observing him. Remember the hair ornament?* Leela had carried the treasures over to the gaddi after school. Since Haruko had left, she had begun spending time at the gaddi, copying the ornaments Munnaji worked on or drawing from imagination, helping with small tasks. She admired the skill and patience with which her father crafted so much beauty. Though he had no intention of teaching his daughter his art, Munnaji tolerated her presence at the ancestral gaddi. Having fathered no son, he knew there would be no one to continue the family craft unless Madanji allowed one of his sons to learn kundan work or one his daughters bore a son who took on the gaddi. Leela had shown the gifts from Haruko to Dadi-sa who had come over to bless her after the evening prayers.

'Japani Jiji says I should learn from Pappaji, Dadi-sa.'

'Yes.' Dadi-sa had nodded in agreement. 'Why can't she learn from you too, just like that girl?' she had asked Munnaji. 'You taught her, why not your own daughter?'

'Ma-sa, it is not your age to turn senile yet.' Munnaji had laughed her off.

Later that evening, Dadi-sa had gone to bed as usual after reading from the *Ramcharitmanas*.

Around midnight, she had woken up Leela's mother. 'I would like to have a paan, Bahu,' she had demanded, 'with gulkand and sweet supari.' She hadn't eaten a paan since she had lost her husband as a young girl.

Leela's mother was bewildered, but had prepared a paan nevertheless, coating the green betel leaf with lime and catechu and filling it with rose preserve and soft areca nuts. Dadi-sa had taken the carefully wrapped leaf, removed the clove holding it together, and popped it into her mouth. After eating it, she had blessed them all, lain back in bed and given up her soul, her mouth sweetened after years of abstinence.

After Munnaji's accident, the incomplete assignments he was working on and the commissions he had accepted had to be completed. Madanji had taken over the work. Unasked, Leela had begun helping at his gaddi. No one had objected. After Haruko, the artisans were used to the presence of a woman at the gaddi. Clad in a loose salwar kameez, her hair in a long braid, Leela appeared there every afternoon. She made herself useful, quietly operating the lathe, cleaning the furnace, filling the carafes with water, making copies of intricate designs for multiple artisans to work on simultaneously. Soon, she was allowed to do simple metalwork, cutting, shaping and polishing metal strips and ornaments. She carried pieces from one master artisan to another, up and down the net of streets, and lingered at the thresholds of the tiny rooms they worked in, quietly observing.

Her father's engraver was the first one to notice her deep interest. One day, he silently handed her the long sharp takua and an inexpensive gold-plated necklace, pointing towards a corner of his room. Leela remained in her corner that entire afternoon, and at the end of it, she handed the piece back engraved with parrots and lotuses, the traditional Jaipur motifs. He nodded at the purity of line and proportion and, from then on, permitted her to work on his pieces from time to time.

Word got around in the artisan community about her dexterity, and other artisans let her help them when overwhelmed with assignments as well, sometimes paying her small sums for the work she did. All the while, Leela observed keenly, learnt unobtrusively. The crafts of etching, enamelling and setting, all interested her. Madanji too heard the bazaar's chatter about his niece's light but firm touch, and the time she spent helping others. He began giving her work at his own gaddi.

'At least this way she will be in front of my eyes and be of use to the family, instead of roaming in the bazaar,' he explained to her mother. 'She has the eyes and hands of Bhai-sa. If she were not a girl, she could be a master artisan. But God plucked our golden grain and left us with the chaff.' He shook his head sadly.

Leela did the work given to her by Madanji, and still managed to find time to assist the master meenakars, kundansaazes and chiteras who worked independently. As she continued her visits and quiet learning of the traditional jewellery crafts, artisans in the bazaar became used to seeing her around, negotiating the maze of streets, slipping in and out of havelis.

The financial situation of Munnaji's family became precarious as time passed and he still lay supine, unable to lift a hand, slipping in and out of the world around him. In the years preceding the accident, he had married his two older daughters off, one after another. Loans had been taken for the lavish ceremonies and dowry. The lenders in the bazaar, the Sarafs, had lent the money without demur. They knew Munnaji was the number-one kundansaaz, always in demand – that he'd repay the loans in no time. But after his accident, as years of expensive medical treatment went by and there was no improvement in his condition, the lenders became concerned. They began visiting in groups and sat around Munnaji's bed in the baithak – the same room where Haruko had recovered. While they commiserated in honeyed words, their shrewd, hungry eyes surrounded him.

'Chh, chh,' they clicked their tongues sympathetically. 'His body was once so full with prosperity and now he is so thin, who would recognize him? How sad it is that the haveli is rented out, with only womenfolk left in the household. Soon you'll be selling the haveli, and the gaddi too. Please don't be embarrassed to tell us when you do. You are our brother, we will buy it ourselves. That way it will remain in the family, for are we not family?' They looked at each other and nodded, agreeing among themselves. 'Yes, yes, we will pay market rate and, after deducting the principal and the interest that you owe us, you'll have enough left for the wedding of this girl who is still a burden on you. Then you and your wife can go to Haridwar and pray to the merciful gods every day.'

They said the same things in different ways each time they visited, praising God's kindness and claiming family bonds, and they visited often. Even with his wandering mind, Munnaji grasped their meaning. Leela saw that his eyes grew anxious, his slurring speech slurred further, his hands trembled when they visited.

One day, after serving the Sarafs tea, she stopped in the doorway of the baithak as they began clicking like deathwatch beetles. 'I am learning kundan work and jewellery making,' she said to them. 'I've already learnt a lot in the past years, and every day I am learning more. Next year, I will reopen the gaddi, and in two years' time I will begin repaying your loans. I will make beautiful jewellery, more beautiful than even Pappaji's. We won't sell the gaddi, we will repay every paisa.' She was breathless towards the end.

Her speech was inevitably talked about in the bazaar. Everyone agreed that the girl who looked so quiet had a long tongue. But it did not hurt her with the artisans – they had all borrowed from the Sarafs and had suffered at their hands. They were pleased that the rich Sarafs were discomfited by the young girl.

It was more than a year since the day she had confronted the Sarafs and, as far as the reopening of the gaddi went, Leela had kept her word. She had been working out of the old gaddi for many months now, but the work she did was as far from Haruko's sheeshphool as Haruko herself was from her.

LEELA CARRIED THE tiffin up the narrow staircase. The stone steps were worn and slippery, and rose at a steep incline to the first and second floors of the haveli. The rooms on both floors faced the inner courtyard, which was dark like a well in the rapidly descending moonless night. The second floor was unoccupied and unlit at night. The old craftsman who rented it used the rooms only during the day, and returned home in the evening to a house his sons had bought in one of the new suburbs. People in the bazaar said he was a fine thewa artist himself, had been felicitated in Delhi, had won national awards for his pieces, but now he occupied his days crafting cheap silver jewellery for one of the fashionable emporiums on M.I. Road. A faint light filtered from under one of the doors on the first floor. Leela knocked. The door opened and, as usual, Manish stepped out, closing the door behind him.

'It's you! You can't leave us alone, can you?' He had very light eyes surrounded by long, spiky lashes. The whole effect was that of a pale, thorny flower.

'I really should, instead of climbing all these stairs with your food. Where is your brother?' She held out the tiffin.

Manish ignored it, taking her hand instead. 'Inside. Doing push-ups and dreaming that someday a girl with eyes like yours will bring him his meal too.' In the faint light, his eyes, the colour of gold mixed with silver, held hers. His warm fingers and palm caressed her soft, brown arm.

'No need for him to dream, I bring both your meals. My mother has asked me to tell you that you both are number one in laziness and, next time, if you don't come to the kitchen downstairs to get your food, I am to let you starve.' She tried to shake his hand off, taking care not to let the tiffin fall.

Manish took the tiffin and placed it on the floor, holding her hand in his, their fingers entwined. Then he pulled her closer, his hands feeling her body through the thin cotton of her shirt. Leela's breasts tingled, her neck prickled and she felt tides surge within.

'No one starves in a place like this, full of delicious savouries.' He brought his face closer to hers. 'But there is little opportunity to taste them.' He held her waist with his two hands and drew her closer still.

A thrill ran through Leela's body and she made a half-hearted attempt to pull away. 'I am sure you are never starved, you are so good at grabbing.'

'*I am not starved, yet I am never sated, such is my fate. When will my luck turn? I am a man who dies of thirst at the banks of a brimming river...*' Manish sang the lines of a popular song.

The sound of a door opening floated up from the dark inner courtyard. Leela shook herself free and bounded down the steps.

A FEW DAYS later, after she had finished reading the headlines from the newspaper to her father, she spoke to him about the lack of fine material to work with. He was more present that day and had asked in his slurred voice whether they planned to organize the annual puja at the gaddi, now that it was open again.

'Yes, we will, Pappaji. But you should see the work Kako-sa gives me – he would never have dared to show you such stuff. How am I to ever make anything good with that second-rate material? He never allows me to make anything original, just gives me cheap stones to set or hollow moulds to cast and fill with lac. Meaningless, profitless work. Most days, I end up firing the ornaments once the enamellers have finished with them. He has seen the engraving and enamelling I do for artisans in the bazaar sometimes. But he just won't let me touch the good pieces.'

'You do as he says, Leela,' her mother, who was rubbing Munnaji's legs with warm oil, interjected. 'It is enough that he lets you work and pays you too. No one in the bazaar will give work to a girl – the work you get from the artisans is because you have his hand over your head. If he draws his hand back, who will shelter you? You have a big mouth. Anyway, in a year or so we'll find a match for you.'

'There's no match for me, I am matchless.' Leela smiled her old lightning smile.

'This girl has a big mouth,' her mother repeated but her father smiled. 'She doesn't go to school and gads about in the market and complains about her elders.'

Leela had stopped attending school after finishing tenth grade. Between the time she spent at the artisans' workshops and the work she needed to do for Madanji, there was no time left for school.

Madanji had remonstrated with her. 'You must go to school, this is an important year. How will you pass?'

'I will write the exams privately, Kako-sa. I will manage,' Leela had replied quietly.

She was working on an earring a jeweller from a neighbouring gaddi had brought earlier in the day. The piece was ill-crafted, the stud too light for the heavy teardrop-shaped dangler which hung askew as a result. Madanji had warned the jeweller that taking the enamelled piece already set with diamonds apart, soldering new links and re-hanging the dangler would ruin it. 'Look here, you'll suffer a loss. The meena will burst and the lac inside the piece will melt at the first touch of flame. The thing will lose its shape altogether. It will become worthless.' But the jeweller was desperate. 'It is ruined already. What use is it with the latkan hanging all wrong?' Leela had been listening. 'Could I try, Kako-sa?' she had asked and Madanji had handed her the piece, repeating his warning that the jeweller would lose money, the piece was beyond salvaging. Leela took the piece apart and corrected the stud by adding a layer of gold to the back to add weight to it. As Madanji spoke to her, she was focussed on joining the two parts together, flicking the flame of the tiny soldering torch, fine and blue like a jacaranda petal, lightly against the open links to seal them. Madanji's voice seemed like a faraway sound to her, carrying little meaning, as she finished the delicate task. 'Look, Kako-sa,' she was jubilant. 'It's done! Not spoilt at all. One rub of the shyan slab and no one can tell there's ever been anything wrong with it.'

Madanji did not give up. He visited her mother a few days later. 'I have tried to explain to her. She is thinking impossible things. She can never be a sunar, no matter what she does. No one will give her work. The work for the gaddi is only to help you out until we find a good boy for her and send her to her own home,' he said.

Leela's mother wiped her eyes. She cried easily these days. Whenever anyone spoke sympathetically, her eyes filled with tears. 'What can I do, Dyor-sa? She looks quiet and obedient, but when her heart is set on something, who can stop her? I have told her that if she does not complete high school, no one will marry her. Boys want educated girls these days. But she listens to me as much as that mortar in the kitchen does.' She sniffed. 'Nobody sees it, but she has always been like this from when she was a small girl, changing from day to day, always doing as she pleased. One day she would want someone to hold her hand and help her cross the narrow rainwater drain in the courtyard, and the next day she would shake her sisters' hands off and run to the school in the main bazaar on her own. Can you imagine, wouldn't cross the mori but crossed the roads by herself ... I couldn't do much with her then either ... Only her Pappaji could, or Ma-sa ... And now Ma-sa is in heaven and her Pappaji is helpless like a child, can't do anything, can hardly understand what is going on...' Her tears flowed freely.

Despite threatening to not let her do any more work for his gaddi if she did not re-join school, Madanji continued to give her work. She was dependable and he paid her less than other artisans, pointing out at every opportunity that he was doing her a favour by letting her work at his gaddi.

Leela's deft handiwork with the earring became known in the bazaar, and problem pieces – those with poor crafting or leaking meena or badly set stones – began coming her way. Jewellers and artisans paid her well for the repairs, better than Madanji did, but Leela knew that repairing defective pieces carried no glory. Master artisans rarely agreed to accept repairs, and all repair-work was prefaced with the customary warning of, 'You will suffer a loss, Brother.' Repairing a faulty piece was time-consuming and reflected little credit on the artisan compared to original crafting. On the other hand, failure to correct a fault would always be remembered: 'He might be an expert jadiya but he ruined my jadau pahunchi, the fine chains fused when he re-set the stones,' an aggrieved jeweller might say, omitting to mention that the row of diamonds adorning the delicate bracelets had not been set straight in the first place and that the jadiya had tried to correct it as best as he could.

Leela was not entirely surprised that the jewellers whose work and investment she salvaged by her deft repairing never commissioned her to craft new pieces. 'You have a housewife's skill to fix and repair. Women are handy at mending, it's a woman's field. And you have time on hand,' they would say to her face, implying that a real artisan, a meenakar or a jadiya or a patwa or any of the other specialized craftsmen would not have the time to correct others' mistakes.

'They think I am only a girl, they don't see the quality of my work,' she complained to her mother, as she hastily ate her lunch of rotis and pickle. It was wedding season, and she had a much work to finish, lightweight pieces with very inferior workmanship which Madanji had given her in bulk to fire and polish.

'They are right, you are only a girl. We don't have the tradition of our girls becoming sunars. Your Kako-sa says so, and your Pappaji used to as well.'

Leela knew her mother was right. Munnaji had never encouraged her. He used to say he had prayed for a son, a child with clever hands to master his craft and advance the family art when Leela was in the womb, and God granted only half his prayer.

'But how about the Japani Jiji? She learnt the craft.'

'She was foreign, she wasn't a sunar, Leela. And however clever she might have been with the kundan and all, that did not make her a sunar.' Her mother rose. 'I am going to see whether the ground-floor tenants will pay the rent today. You go ask the old man on the second floor before going back to the gaddi.'

Leela finished her lunch and washed the utensils in the washing area in the inner courtyard. Drying her hands on her dupatta, she sprinted up the steep stairs.

'Tayaji, namaste,' she called out, standing at the door.

The white-haired artisan raised his head from the silver knick-knack he was working on. 'How are you, Beti?'

'I am all right, Tayaji. Ma asked me to collect the rent.'

'Yes, yes, of course.' He stretched his arm for the cotton kurta hanging from a hook on the wall.

'I'll get it for you.' Leela handed it to him.

He drew out crisp, new notes, counted them carefully and handed them over to her. 'Tell me, Beti, is it true that you've repaired some fairly bad work recently?'

Leela blushed. She felt the unfairness that he of all people, should bring up the repair-work, hold it against her. He himself made cheap silver baubles, a downfall of some magnitude for a top thewa-maker, and yet he thought of her as a repairer, inferior to a real artisan.

'Yes, Tayaji, I mended a necklace, a heavy kanthi. The meena on one end was spoilt. I did my best. I don't get the chance to make top-quality kundan, so I turn my hand to what is given to me. In any case, ornaments are made so that their beauty can be enjoyed by everyone who sees them. If a mistake mars the beauty, is there anything wrong in correcting it?'

'Nothing wrong, nothing at all. Repairing the mistakes of others to restore beauty is work which deserves blessings.' Leela blushed again. 'I asked because I wanted to see whether you would like to learn thewa. It is blinding work and slow, but the beauty of a finished piece is something to behold.'

Leela stood still. The old man was a Soni, a true artist from the clan of sunars, and he was offering to teach her. Except for Haruko, no one had taught her willingly. She had merely been tolerated.

'It is not easy work, you understand? Not quick and showy, no jewels and colours to help hide flaws. Only pure gold, and what your eyes can see and your hands can do with it. My own sons won't do it.'

'Why, Tayaji?'

'They did not wish to spend time on learning it, Beti. They wanted an easy life – to work in offices, be babus. They would tell their mother that they did not want to go blind over trinkets. I stopped teaching them, left Pratapgarh where my clan had lived and practised our art for four generations, and came to Jaipur so I could send them to college. Now they spend their days going blind over files and computers.'

'Why do you make these silver things, Tayaji?'

'I must do something with my hands, Beti, and I can't do the thewa work alone. Here, there are not too many who understand it. They like things that shine and flash like avaz ki jadai or meena. The effort required to craft thewa is beyond them, they don't have the patience for it. I thought, since you saw the soul of beauty in damaged ornaments, you might have the patience to learn...'

'I have patience, Tayaji. Whatever I know, I have learnt by watching. No one here has ever wanted to teach me, not even Pappaji...'

'Don't hold it against them, Beti. Your biradari does not allow a girl to be taught these things. My own clan does not involve daughters or daughters-in-law in our art. My grandfather only taught his middle son, my father, the rest he considered unworthy. Now there are only few who know my art and even fewer who want to learn.'

'I want to learn. I saw a thewa necklace once, at the big gaddi in the main bazaar. It was very finely worked and its glass glowed like jewels.'

'No hard stones can compete with the brittle beauty of glass, Beti. It is so fragile, a glance can mar its beauty. Come in the morning tomorrow, and we will begin.'

Leela nodded.

On the landing of the first floor an arm blocked her path. It was Manish. He quickly pulled her inside the room.

'I came to pick up a box of samples I had forgotten and am rewarded for my forgetfulness.' He held her tight and kissed her on the mouth. 'Better than cool sugarcane juice on this hot day!'

Leela wriggled out of his arms. 'I need to hurry. I got talking to Tayaji.'

'But won't stop to talk to me? Such is my fate.'

'Don't start singing that silly song, I really don't like it. Tayaji thinks I can be a sunar.'

'How does that matter when you are already an ornament?' Manish caught hold of the free ends of her dupatta, holding her back.

'You think you are very clever. Ma will come looking for me soon. Let's see what you'll say to her.'

'I will tell her that she and your Pappaji are true sunars, together they made an ornament like you!'

'Shameless! She will slap you so hard you will forget your address.'

'If I do, I will follow the scent of your body and reach here. Or I will ask the doctor I met today for it! He knows the address of this haveli – he said he used to visit many years ago to treat some Japani or Cheeni girl.'

'You met Dr Prakash?' Leela turned towards Manish.

'Yes, you know him?'

'He treated Haruko Jiji when her leg was broken – I told you about her.'

'The one who was so clever she knew years ago that I would marry you and gave you the sheeshphool for our wedding?'

'You are stupid. She designed his wedding card.'

'As a fee for healing her leg?'

'No, as a fee for breaking her heart.'

She pulled her dupatta out of Manish's grasp and ran down the stairs.

THE NEXT MORNING, Tayaji came earlier than usual. Leela saw him enter the haveli as she prepared an elaborate breakfast of halwa and parathas in the kitchen.

It was the month of Sawan, when married women returned to their parental home for the traditional annual visit, and Munnaji's two sisters were visiting along with their children. Leela's sisters hadn't come, however. Her elder sister was pregnant with her first child. It was early days, and her mother-in-law had refused to send her. 'She will come to you for delivery in a few months,' she had said to Leela's mother who had called on her with boxes of sweets, 'until then, it is better she stays here.' It was decided that Leela's other sister should visit at that time too – it was not possible for her to be spared from her sasural twice in one year. Leela's mother had bowed her head. What could she say? She had given her daughters away and had no right over them. She had to accept whatever their in-laws decided.

Leela's mother was chatting with Munnaji's sisters, talking over the situation of the family, her worries about Leela, about Munnaji's uncertain grip on things around him. Leela saw the old manner in which her mother took her ease by the door of the inner room, her sister-in-law massaging her beautiful long hair with perfumed oil, and felt a lightness of heart she hadn't felt in a while. She filled a small bowl with halwa and covered it with a cotton handkerchief. Then she spread some pickle on a paratha and made a roll.

'Breakfast is ready, Bua-sa,' she called as she emerged from the kitchen. 'Please eat quickly, otherwise everything will get cold. I need to run.' She ate the rolled up paratha as she went up to the third floor with the bowl of halwa in her hand. 'Tayaji.' She entered the small room. 'I have brought some halwa.' She uncovered the bowl and placed it before him. The room filled with the sweet fragrance of roasted flour and ghee and sugar.

Tayaji smiled. 'Good, good. Very auspicious to begin the first lesson with a sweetened mouth.'

That morning, and every morning for the next few months, Tayaji showed her the technique of thewa, of mixing terracotta with oil and chemicals to make the base, fine freehand etching, cutting the gold foil for a filigree-like effect, and affixing it on to polished glass. He taught her the elaborate traditional motifs of women training parakeets and palanquin processions, tiger hunts and court dances, and allowed her to experiment with designs and etching techniques from the book sent by Haruko. She learnt to heat glass at the right temperature for fusing pure gold leaf and to handle gold leaf with precision.

'What I am teaching you took me years to perfect, Beti – the right mix for the base, the right temperature, the right technique for shining the glass,' Tayaji told her. 'My grandfather was secretive about his techniques. He used to work in the dead of night so that no one could spy on him and emulate his method. He did not teach everything even to my father. So I had to experiment and try. There was much wastage initially, because the foil which is cut away is useless, too thin to be melted or reused. With accurate measuring and finer etching tools, I reduced wastage.'

Leela spent as much time as she could take out from her work to learn the thewa processes. She was mesmerized by its glass-and-gold beauty, more delicate and artful even than kundan.

'Thewa is the ultimate fruit of jewellery craft, Beti.' Tayaji would say. 'To convert humble glass and meagre gold foil into such fragile beauty requires the highest form of swarankari. It goes beyond the art of ornament making – it is the art of life itself. To fuse the pure with the frail without melting one or breaking the other.'

SAWAN WAS OVER, and Leela's mother prepared seasonal gifts of sweets and clothes, bangles and toys, for Leela's aunts and to send to her sisters' homes.

The night before they left, Leela's aunts sat beside Munnaji's cot and complained about her ways. 'Who will marry a girl who runs about all day in the bazaar or sits bent like an old woman among craftsmen? Madan Bhai-sa ought not to encourage her by giving her work, and you should tell her to close the gaddi down. It is not for girls to run our ancestral gaddi,' they said to Munnaji as he lay helpless, looking from one to another. 'We have to hear things at our in-laws. Everyone says you are going against the biradari, allowing Leela to break the rules of the community.'

Leela entered with glasses of cold milk.

'You must stop all this, Leela.' The older of the two turned to her. 'You barely passed your examinations last year. Now you must stay at home and help your mother with the household chores.'

'And where will we find the money to run the household itself, Bua-sa? Who will bear the expense of Badi JiJi's delivery?' Leela's elder sister had to deliver her first-born at her parent's home as tradition required, and the expense on ceremonies and gifts would be heavy. 'The work I do brings money so we can buy medicines for Pappaji and seasonal gifts for you so you don't have to hear worse things at your sasural.' Looking at her father's stricken eyes, she added, 'Once Pappaji is better, we will have nothing to worry about.'

She left the room. Thereafter, her aunts mentioned the unfettered tongue of Munnaji's youngest at every family gathering.

THE DAY LEELA fused the carefully carved, paper-thin sheet of gold on to sparkling glass to complete her first thewa piece – a pendant Tayaji had set her to work on – was a day of jubilation and revealed beauty.

Tayaji examined her work carefully. 'This is good,' he said. 'You'll do better soon, but this is good for now.'

Tayaji gave the piece to one of the bazaar jewellers to sell. He had bought the material for the first piece himself, but neither he nor Leela had money to buy more. Until the piece was sold, Leela practised on silver foil and cheap glass.

A few days later, Tayaji entered the haveli and called Leela. 'Here, this is prasad,' he said, handing her a box of laddus. 'First piece sold, and at a good price too.' He took some money out of his pocket. 'Take your first real artisan's fee. I bought more material for you with the rest.'

'Please take this as your guru dakshina, Tayaji,' Leela said.

He shook his head. 'Not now. I will take it when your lessons are over. There's a long way to go.'

Leela continued with her training. The jeweller who had agreed to keep the first piece at his gaddi and pay only when it was sold, offered to buy the pieces she crafted outright. Leela did not mention the thewa work to anyone, silently handing the additional money to her mother after the sale of each piece.

Madanji soon learnt about it from the talk in the bazaar. He came around to complain to Leela's mother. 'She is wasting time making worthless glass baubles and selling them in the bazaar. She is the daughter of the finest kundansaaz in the whole of Jaipur. How could you let her do that? It is taking time away from the work at our gaddi too.'

'What can I say, Dyor-sa? I have never been able to do much with her, she is so stubborn. Besides, the old man gives her all the money, never keeps a rupee for his fee or the cost of running the furnace or anything. Because of the money, we could get the haveli whitewashed after so many years.

Your Bhai-sa looked so happy! You should have seen how he kept smiling and sniffing at the smell of fresh whitewash...' She covered her tearful eyes with the free end of her sari.

Manish too heard about her pieces being sold in the market. 'It is one thing to help your uncle, but quite another to make and sell ornaments like a common sunar of the bazaar.'

'There is nothing common about being a sunar. Besides, I only work with Tayaji.'

'Leela, don't argue pointlessly. You only call him Tayaji. He is not your father's elder brother. Anyway, you'll have to stop all this sooner or later. I am due for promotion, and then I can talk to my parents about our marriage.'

'You are too fast, take care or you'll fall over your feet! Who said I want to marry you?'

'Shut up. Who else will marry such a wayward girl?' Manish squeezed her roughly and kissed her smiling mouth.

'Someone who doesn't think a sunar is common.'

'Why would anyone think about a sunar when they can think about you, you witch?'

Leela ran away, laughing.

ONE DAY, AS she worked on a necklace, her first big thewa piece, she mentioned Haruko's sheeshphool to Tayaji.

'Looking at it makes me forget whether it is day or night, Tayaji.'

'That's a real ornament then, Beti. Its beauty dims all else.'

'I will bring it for you to see.'

'After we are done with the necklace, Beti. I don't want any shadow to fall on the work you are doing now. You mustn't try to string a pearl and set a sapphire at the same time.'

Leela nodded. The day after the necklace was finished to their satisfaction, Leela brought the hair ornament over for him to see. He ran his fingers over the gloriously coloured surface, smooth under the translucent veneer of enamel, and admired the flawless shape and perfectly set stones.

'This is a masterpiece. Who made it?'

'The Japani Jiji I told you about, the one who stayed with us and taught me. When she was leaving, she gave this to me and said if I could make another one like this, I should write to her...'

'I see. The gold and diamonds and rubies are all very expensive, though. No one in the bazaar will give you and me credit, Beti – a silversmith and a girl have no position in the jeweller's market. You wouldn't want to sell this, would you?' Leela shook her head. 'How about your Kako-sa then? Would he put up the money?'

Leela shook her head again, 'He says I should not try to be a sunar...'

'He is right, Beti. Why should you try when you already are one?'

Tears welled in Leela's eyes, 'You think so, Tayaji?'

'I know that, Beti. Do you want to try this one in thewa? We will have to alter the design though.'

'Yes, Tayaji. I have always wanted to make one as fine as this. In thewa, it would be an original, not a replica. I think Haruko Jiji would like that.'

THEY BEGAN IN earnest as soon as the money from the necklace Leela had crafted was in hand.

Tayaji brought over a piece of old Venetian glass, a beautiful peach in colour. 'This is left over from back when I used to still do fine work.' He rubbed it with a soft muslin cloth and wrapped it carefully in a bit of velvet.

They discussed the design. The two styles, thewa and kundan-meena being so disparate, it was important to plan the sheeshphool carefully to retain a sense of harmony, a shared inspiration between Haruko's and Leela's ornaments. Leela drew the iris-jasmine Haruko had imagined to scale, and tried a few variations. Tayaji agreed that the glass base should be cut in the shape of the flower. Leela worked an elaborate pattern of fantastical flowers to be finely etched in gold leaf for mounting on the peach glass. She was keen to try enamel on the gold-leaf flowers, but hesitated suggesting such a departure from the traditional craft to the old artisan. She managed to mix enamel in a shade of pink, like the evening clouds in Sawan, and showed it to him hesitantly. To her surprise, he looked at the colour with interest.

'Yes, it will connect the two flowers, but the meena will not stay without deeper grooves and it requires firing, Beti. We can certainly try. Perhaps you can deepen the grooves where you want to apply it? The enamel is light enough, so who knows, it might stay. But don't try it on gold straightaway.'

Leela practised on silver foil and scraps of gold, thinning the enamel so that it was like paint on the fine metal leaf. The months it took to design and craft the ornament were a period of intense concentration for Leela. Though she had only a couple of hours in the morning to actually work on it, she went about the whole day resolving questions of detail and design in her head.

Her mother complained of her preoccupation. 'You let the milk boil over again today. And I can't rely on you to even cook a simple dal without forgetting salt or coriander,' she scolded her. 'The next couple of nights I will be at the temple for the nightlong prayers. I don't know whether you'll be able to take care of your Pappaji, give him his dinner...'

Leela remained silent, but the next day she returned early from the gaddi and helped her mother prepare food. When her mother went to bathe and change for the prayers, she went upstairs with the tiffin.

'You are always in a hurry. What is it this time?' Manish held her by the arm as she turned away.

'Ma is going for akhand kirtan at the temple. I need to give Pappaji his dinner and make sure he is comfortable for the night.'

'So she will be gone the whole night? You will remember to close the doors carefully?'

'Of course. Let me go.'

She ran down the steps. Her mother had fasted the whole day in preparation for the prayers, and she warmed some milk for her. Then she served roti, kadhi and saag for her father in a platter and carried it over to the baithak. She propped Munnaji against the bolster pillows and covered his neck and chest with a soft cotton cloth, feeding him small morsels carefully.

Her mother came in to touch Munnaji's feet before leaving for the temple. She wore a red-and-yellow bandhej sari, and fresh vermilion gleamed on her forehead and in the parting of her hair. She looked like she used to in the old days, before the sudden tragedy transformed her.

'Did you drink the milk, Ma?' Leela asked through the lump in her throat.

'Yes. Close the door properly.'

After feeding Munnaji, Leela wiped his face, gave him his medicines and settled him for the night, propping the bolsters around him. She ate a hurried meal in the kitchen and tidied up.

She was washing up at the tap outside the kitchen, when a shadow fell over her. Manish stood in the inner courtyard. 'So careless, you did not shut the door.' He came closer.

Leela rose. Droplets of water fell from her wet face on to her kurta. 'I locked the street door. I didn't know you would come prowling.'

'Didn't you, Leela?' He held her hands. They stood in the wet area around the tap.

'We'll both fall, it is slippery here.'

'I am holding you.' Manish took her in his arms. 'I have waited for so long.' He touched her ear, her cheek, her mouth with his fingers.

There were tenants in the rooms across the courtyard. Leela could see light filtering from under the doors. She guided Manish to the kitchen. Closing the door softly, she spread the cotton floor seat that her mother used for praying in the middle of the kitchen, and there, among the saucepans and setting curd and smell of food, Manish caressed her. He kissed her and sucked at her breasts and entered her with a breath-taking suddenness. He held her legs up and bit her as he came.

Afterwards, he lay by her side, holding her to him. 'Your first time, I could feel it. Did you like it? Did you like me inside you?'

Leela said nothing. She had felt dazed, and then a sharp pain had made her tremble when he pushed inside her. He kept his arms wrapped around her, pressing her naked body to his, the strap of his watch digging into her back.

She pushed him away from her gently. 'I need to go check on Pappaji. You should leave too, the tenants might hear something.'

Manish kissed her again and again before finally rising. He pulled on his clothes and, opening the kitchen door carefully, left. Leela got up too and went to the bathroom. There was blood. She cleaned herself and, putting on a loose nightgown, went back to the kitchen. She rolled up the floor seat and put it away. A powerful craving for something sweet came upon her, her insides churned. She did not remember feeling this hungry ever and ate spoonful after spoonful of the brown, crumbly cane sugar until her lips stuck and her mouth turned sour.

THE WORK ON the glass-and-gold sheeshphool progressed slowly.

After the painstaking etching and delicate shading with the enamel was complete, Leela washed the glass with a mild acid and polished it until it shone like a jewel. Next, she mounted the wafer-thin gold etching on to the glass, carefully cutting away the superfluous foil over several days. Finally, she backed the glass with a thin sheet of silver and soldered a pin to it.

The day the ornament was finished, the first real shower fell and the smell of dry earth drinking the nectar-like drops after months of heat rose all around. Leela placed the finished ornament in a velvet case and carried it over to a photographer in the next street.

'I need the photos by email,' she told him when he had finished taking shots of it from different angles. 'I have to send them to a foreign lady.'

She had carefully composed a brief email: *Namaste Haruko Jiji, Leela this side. I made the sheeshphool. It is same but different. I made with thewa. I hope you like it.* She sent it with the photos attached and included the number of the cheap mobile phone she had recently bought.

A few days after she sent the email, Haruko called. Leela was at the gaddi, repairing a set of bangles.

'It is simply marvellous!' Haruko said of the piece. 'What is that beautiful base made of?' Leela explained in detail. Haruko was fascinated by the glass-and-gold fusion, the fine, tracery-like engraving. 'I want you to make more of this thewa stuff, Leela. It is sensational! Can you make brooches, pendants?'

'I can make all. Anything. But it takes long, long time.' She told Haruko about her father's accident and the necessity of working on Madanji's assignments. 'I must do work for Madan Kako-sa ... Bad quality things, but it is for money.'

'That's terrible. I am so sorry to hear,' Haruko said.

'Yes,' Leela replied. 'It is very, very bad. Been bad for years.'

'Well, at least you need not work on Madanji's assignments any more. I am hiring you. You will work for me now.'

'No, Jiji. I am sunar now. I work my own gaddi, but I make only for you.'

'Perfect. I like that! Email me your bank details, I will wire money. Plan ten different pieces. I'd like to see different designs. And if the rest of your work is as good as this one, we'll have our joint collection next spring.' Leela could hear the smile in Haruko's voice. 'Haruko-Leela sounds cool for the name of a jewellery collection, doesn't it?'

Leela returned home on winged feet. She kept the conversation with Haruko to herself until the money she sent was credited into Munnaji's bank account. She was surprised at the amount. The bank manager himself called her. 'It is a big sum. Very big. We need to complete the paperwork,' he said. The money was sufficient for her to buy material for several pieces, begin repaying the loans – sufficient to no longer accept bazaar work.

She told her mother and father that evening. 'Haruko Jiji has sent so much money. Finally our gaddi is independent again. We need not look to Kako-sa any more. And we can ask the ground-floor people to find another place so that Badi Jiji and the others will be comfortable when they arrive next month.'

Munnaji's eyes remained vacant, but her mother grumbled, 'You have such a long tongue, Leela. What will the biradari say? Cutting off from Dyor-sa's gaddi ... setting up in the bazaar as if you are a sunar.'

'I am a sunar, Ma. Everyone knows that now. And the community will not pay back the loans or pay for Jiji's delivery. We must do what we must do. If Kako-sa had treated me fairly, like an artist, I would not have gone to Haruko Jiji.'

She told Madanji the next day. 'I will complete the work on hand, but I can't take any more, Kako-sa. Haruko Jiji wants me to work full-time on designing and crafting with her.'

Madanji was furious. 'You are going too far, Leela. This is against our tradition, against the way our elders set for us. You are bringing disrepute to us all.'

'I don't think so, Kako-sa. When I did the inferior quality work for you and repair-work for the bazaar folk, perhaps then I was bringing disrepute on Pappaji's gaddi. But now I will only do good work with good material. I will take the gaddi forward.'

'You speak like a person who has lost all sense. No one will give work to you here, no one will regard you as a sunar. You are just working for a foreign girl who learnt from us.'

'Everyone learns from someone, Kako-sa. And I am not working for anyone, I am partner with Haruko Jiji. We will design and make together. Our gaddi is not dependent on anyone any more, only on my skill as a sunar.'

'You are taking advantage of your father's incapacity, Leela,' Madanji shouted.

'And what were you doing all these years, Kako-sa, when you paid me less than everyone else, even the most raw of youngsters who could barely solder things straight?'

Madanji pointed to the door, his hand shaking.

LEELA FINISHED THE remainder of the work she had on hand diligently, and delivered it on time to Madanji's gaddi and to others. The news spread quickly about how Munnaji's daughter was disgracing him by setting up independently in the bazaar. Madanji was the most vocal of her critics. 'She is throwing dust on our turbans, rubbing our noses into dung,' he said to anyone who cared to listen.

Only Tayaji was pleased. 'You are going to do good work, Beti. No worries now about money, and no need to bother with pedestrian bazaar work. People will come to you for fine work.'

'All because of the thewa you taught me, Tayaji. Please take your dakshina now.'

'Later, later. Once the foreigner likes the things you make, then you will be on a sure footing. Don't worry, I will take my teaching fee, otherwise the skills I taught you will not be fruitful for you.' He laughed. 'Now, we must not waste time. From tomorrow onwards, work on the style and designs. We need to finalize those before we can come to an estimate of the materials required. Ten pieces is not a small number – especially of the fine quality the maker of that kundan sheeshphool would expect. You will have to work harder than ever before, Beti.'

Leela nodded and touched the old artist's feet.

IN THE WEEKS that followed, Leela worked long and hard, often returning home just to eat and go back to the gaddi to work. A few weeks after setting up independently, she was at the gaddi late one evening. The street was bathed in the soft golden glow of a late winter evening. The forty-day chill that began in December had ended, but the days were still short. Leela glanced up from her work as the street door of the gaddi opened. Manish stood at the threshold. Since her conversation with Haruko and the upheavals it had created, they hadn't had an opportunity to talk.

'Have you come to order ornaments for your bride?' She smiled happily at him.

'Yes,' Manish said. He did not step inside the gaddi. 'Where have you been, Leela?'

'Here, where else?'

'I get news of you from the savoury shops and the sunar shops in the street these days. Everyone's talking of you in the bazaar.'

Leela kept her smiling eyes fixed on him. 'So? You will have a famous bride.'

'Not famous, infamous. Madanji told me all about your quarrel with him. He is your uncle, Leela, he has helped you.'

Leela looked away. Her eyes no longer smiled. 'I worked for him when I was in need. He paid me as little as he could get away with. I was his niece then too.'

'Do you have no fear? What if that foreign woman decides not to help you? What will you do then?'

'She is not helping me out of pity. My work is good and she likes it. Unlike Kako-sa, she is fair, she treats me as an equal, as a skilled sunar. And if she does not like my work any more, I know there are others out there who will.'

'So you have chosen to have a rift with the family because you want to make ornaments like a common craftsman? My parents would never agree to our marriage if this goes on, Leela.'

The brief, pastel-coloured dusk of late Paush was over and night had fallen in the street. Manish stood half lost in the darkness outside. To Leela, he seemed to be poised at the mouth of a dark tunnel. She glanced down at her desk and adjusted the clips holding the design she was working on.

'Is all this so important, Leela? Is it so important to be a sunar?'

Leela picked up her mechanical pencil and turned the desk lamp on. A bright shaft of light illuminated the detailed design she was working on.

'There is nothing more important,' she said.

YURI

I LAY STRETCHED ON the tatami in the living room, a cushion under my elbow. The Sunday papers were strewn on the floor. I looked around the small sunlit room and my gaze rested on Yuri. She sat working on her laptop at the writing table, neat piles of medical bills, reports, official-looking documents at her elbow. She had cut her hair very short, in a style that swept away from her face leaving her fragile jawline and neck exposed. In the clear light of the July afternoon, her face looked thin, her temples and cheeks hollow, her cheekbones casting translucent shadows. I was surprised.

'You've lost weight, Yuri. You look so thin,' I said.

'You've just noticed, Meenu-chan?' Yuri smiled gently. 'All my clothes are loose. I am at my lowest weight ever these last few months.'

'How could I have known? You haven't been around these past months.' I regretted the resentment in my tone as soon as I spoke. I knew the multiple stresses that had fallen heavy on Yuri lately.

'I know, and I am sorry, Meenu-chan,' Yuri said in her soft voice. 'This has been difficult for you. New city, new work among strangers, and no one to find comfort with. The thought of your loneliness has troubled me. Suppose we go out for lunch today?'

My phone beeped. It was Hajime, asking what time I would be over for lunch. 'Ummm ... But isn't there a deadline for submitting these insurance claims?'

'They can wait. I will do them tomorrow. Today we shall enjoy our lunch, perhaps at one of the nice restaurants by the Kamogawa. It has been a while since we went out, had some saké, looked at each other. I will just save these documents.'

Yuri began tapping into her laptop. I typed a hurried message to Hajime: *Can't come.* My phone rang with a symphony of beeps as Hajime sent one message after another in quick succession before I could turn off the ringer. *Why??? What happened? I have gone all out – tempura, fried bean curd skin, shiitake mushrooms. Come on, Meena!!*

'Someone is eagerly trying to catch your attention, Meenu-chan?' Yuri asked, smiling.

My cheeks burned. 'Folk from Uni. There's programme planning going on.' The message light on my phone was blinking again. Hajime was not one to give up easily.

I FIRST CAME across Hajime in my early days at the Kyoto University. I had transferred from Tokyo and had been at the university for a couple of months, but matters related to my fellowship were still unresolved. I went to the administrative department every day, but I could get no clear idea when my scholarship funds would be released. That day, too, I was walking towards the School of Humanities at the Yoshida campus after my daily pilgrimage to the administrative department. There was a group of Japanese students crossing the quad ahead of me, one of them holding forth animatedly on modern literature. His eager manner contrasted sharply with the soft, restrained ways of the others surrounding him, and I couldn't help listening with interest. 'Modern literature is not the key to the modern world,' he was saying. 'One is a labyrinth in which the other is lost. You have to figure out which is which. This cannot be done by holding yourself apart, like the sage who peacefully contemplates a Zen garden. You have to get involved, like the landscaper who designs the garden, examines the stream, places sounding stones, plants and warps the trees, and who therefore understands what went into creating its beauty.' His Japanese had an unfamiliar accent. The group reached the International Centre for Research Studies. The speaker turned around and cast an inquiring look at me as the others filed inside. I realized that I had been so engrossed in listening that I had followed them, leaving my own department behind. I blushed and muttered an apology, turning back quickly, but not before I saw the amusement in his eyes.

A few days later, I saw him again, sitting down to a solitary lunch at Camphora Café just outside the gates of the university. On an impulse, I approached his table, tray in hand. 'Do you mind?' I began.

'You have followed me here too?' he said in English, and the reason for the unfamiliar accent in his Japanese became instantly clear – he spoke with an American accent. He laughed at me as I stood wavering. 'You make an interesting backlit picture, but won't you sit down? I wouldn't want your pasta to go cold. The day's special is ramen though.'

I set my tray on the table. 'I'm sorry to intrude,' I began.

'I don't think you are though! In any event, I am very pleased to be intruded upon! You are from India?' I smiled. 'Where in India?' he asked.

'Have you been to India?'

'No, unfortunately not, but I fully intend to. And soon.'

'I'll tell you when you've visited India. No point in doing so now.'

'I haven't been to the moon either, but I still like to keep track of its phases, eclipses and cycles. I hope you do not disapprove!'

'Not at all, I lay no claim on the moon. You can indulge in as much idle curiosity at its expense as you wish.'

He laughed. 'Introductions seem a bit lame now that you have been following me all over Kyodai, but I would love to know what to call you. I am Hajime Toshiba.'

'Meena. I have transferred from Tokyo Uni for a comparative study project. You?'

'I teach modern literary theory at the ICRS.'

'Oh. I'm so sorry ... I didn't realize you were a professor.'

'Only an associate professor and on contract. Does that make you feel less sorry?'

YURI'S STEPMOTHER HAD passed away after a brief illness early last winter, leaving her father to manage his loneliness and the ryokan in Nara as best as he could. Not long after, he was diagnosed with cancer of the stomach. He was admitted to the Kyoto Prefecture Hospital and Yuri had travelled from Tokyo to see him. She had expected to spend a few weeks there, but his condition had deteriorated rapidly and her visit had to be extended. She had returned to Tokyo more than a month later, only to resign from her job and apply for leave of absence from her Master's programme at Tokyo University. Her father's prognosis was not optimistic, but there was no clarity on how long life would linger.

Without Yuri, I was adrift in Tokyo. I tried to continue as before, going to the university, working part time in the library, and returning every evening to the apartment in Kasuga that Yuri and I had shared for almost four years. Over weekends, I took solitary walks in the Himarikyu or the imperial gardens, watched the crowds in Ginza, cooked for myself. Yuri tried to come up once in a while, but her hands were full with her father and helping with the ryokan.

'Come to Kyoto, Meenu-chan,' she had said. 'You have been in Tokyo all this while, living in another city would be good. Kyoto is the real Japan, so beautiful and old.'

I talked to my programme director and began applying to universities in and around Kyoto. The day after my fellowship offer from Kyoto University was confirmed, I left Tokyo forfeiting the notice-period rent and leaving our modest furniture behind for the landlord to do as they pleased with.

Being in Kyoto was like my initial days in Tokyo all over again, when I had felt thrown into the stream and left out of the flow at the same time. I knew no one and Yuri was away, spending most of her time between the hospital and the ryokan. I tried to find my feet, organize my life. I had learnt Japanese in the last few years, and that helped. I found a studio apartment on Eiden line, not far from Kyoto University, bought the necessary household items on sale from Takashimaya, and found a local grocery shop which stocked pulses and spices. I learnt the train route to Kyodai, walked around the Yoshida campus, orienting myself with the help of the famous clock tower, memorized locations of my research director's office, the library, the students' co-op. I also found a part-time job from an advertisement on the students' bulletin board. It was three days a week, from seven to nine in the evening, at a shop selling books, games and music. The advertisement had listed proficiency in Japanese as essential, and the owner had looked at me with dismay when I had told him that I had come for the interview. But he was impressed with my Tokyo-accented Japanese, hiring me on the spot. The job turned out to be far more useful than I had thought initially, as my fellowship funds were held up.

I had sent emails to my sisters, telling them about moving to Kyoto, the new project, about the famed university, attaching a picture of the iconic camphor tree in the Yoshida campus. Predictably, there was no response. They had stopped writing to me or responding to my calls in the past three years or so.

AFTER COMPLETING MY initial research work at Tokyo University, I had applied for another research grant. I had no wish to return home. I had begun enjoying Tokyo and wanted to stay on. Also, there was Yuri. I was accepted as a fellow for comparative studies in Japanese literature, but my family continued to insist that I return. The neighbour's son had completed his medical studies and they wanted me to come back, get married.

Yuri had held me close after a particularly stormy call with my mother. 'Please go, Meenu-chan, if you wish to. You have others whose love matters. The mountains are for those with wings of wind, I have feet of earth. I will bear it.' But she had clung to me, pulling me on to her lap, tears spilling from her eyes.

I had kissed her. 'I won't leave you, Yuri. I belong with you,' I had said. 'How can I go back?'

And it was true. I couldn't bear the thought of marrying my neighbour, couldn't imagine living with him, sharing a bed, his dry hands on my body.

When shouting over Skype calls could not persuade me to return, my mother and younger sister had travelled to Tokyo. Despite the recent stresses, I wanted to see them. It had been such a long time. I wanted my mother to stroke my hair and complain how rough they had become, and for my sister to gossip about her friends.

I shifted Yuri and my futons to the living area, and prepared the single bedroom in our tiny flat for them, with fresh sheets and flowers in a vase. I spent the morning cooking a meal of dal and rice, fried okra and potatoes, and yoghurt with crushed mint for them.

They were tired from the ten-hour flight, but my mother began her campaign the moment she saw me at the airport. She ignored the slender pine trees lining the road from Narita, the futuristic, piled-up cityscape of Tokyo, the clear summer sky.

'Why do you want to live here all alone, where no one even knows your language?' she had asked, again and again. 'Why won't you come back, marry Prakash, live close to us?'

I was unable to say why I could not, why the thought of marrying in the neighbourhood, bearing the doctor's children, attending family functions increased my darkness.

'You can work in the university there,' my mother had said. 'It is so close to our home. They are such a progressive family, you know. The boy, he will allow you to teach at the university. They have waited for you all these years, and so have we. What is the matter? Everyone knows that you are to return this year. They are preparing for the marriage. Even the jewellery has been bought...'

She had asked my sister to show pictures on her phone of the engagement ring, the wedding necklace and saris.

'Is there someone else?' my sister had asked in a whisper. 'You can tell me.'

It continued hour after hour. Towards evening, we were all exhausted. My mother and sister rested in the bedroom. I sat alone in the living room.

When Yuri returned, she found me sprawled on the futon in the darkening room, crying. She held me in her arms, caressing my face, running her fingers down my back. 'Don't, Meenu-chan,' she said, 'just don't.' She cradled me close and kissed me deeply on the mouth.

I raised my eyes and saw my sister standing very still in the doorway. Our eyes met in the shadowy room, she averted hers and turned back inside. Moments later, I heard the sickening sound of flesh striking against flesh from the bedroom. I rushed inside to find my mother hitting her forehead with the heel of her palm, again and again, moaning through her clenched teeth. Her glass bangles cracked and her wrist and forehead oozed blood as she continued hitting herself, my sister making ineffectual efforts to hold back her arm.

They left two days later, my mother refusing to look at me or speak to me the whole time.

'You'll see. They will have nothing to do with me now. They won't speak to me, I will not be mentioned in the family,' I told Yuri.

'That is not possible. They love you so much, they are so close to you. They have always thought of you, worried about you,' Yuri countered. 'This is momentary.'

I remained silent. I knew it was because they had loved me in that way, that they would have nothing to do with me now. The day the neighbour's son got married was the last time my sisters had spoken to me. *Our mother won't allow food to be cooked today, won't switch the lights on in the house. It is as if someone has died.* I had understood. I had tried hard to ignore the unbearable loneliness which welled up inside me.

WHEN I HAD walked up to Hajime in the Camphora Café that afternoon, I did not know that I was keeping afloat with my last resources. Only afterwards, when he became a part of my days and the dark floods receded, did I realize how close I was to going under. It was after meeting him that I finally began noticing Kyoto, the softness of its air, the tranquil Kamo which flowed, shallow and clear, through the city.

Hajime was surprised that I had not really seen Kyoto, that I had only caught glimpses of the city from train windows, riding up and down the Eiden line.

'It's unbelievable! We must remedy this ignorance immediately. Not a day to lose. Kyoto is exceptional, classical and modern at the same time. You have got to see the temples and the old houses, the peace of the Arashiyama Bamboo Grove and the Philosopher's Walk. And this is perfect weather. You have a bike?'

I shook my head. I had looked at bicycles in the shops around Kawabata-dori, but the ones I liked were expensive and I was not sure how long it would be before the matter of my fellowship would be resolved. With the lease and other expenses of moving, I was conscious of my depleting bank account.

'I can't afford a nice one, and I won't buy a cheap one.'

'Can't afford?' Hajime raised an eyebrow. 'Aren't you on a ridiculously liberal fellowship for all the back-breaking work you supposedly did at Tokyo University? Is there a hidden vice on which you've managed to squander it all?'

'The fellowship money has not yet been released. It's all a bit confusing, like the mysterious churning of the universe that I can't quite follow.'

'How would you? You have been busy following me. Which, by the way, I fully approve of. But the fellowship issue must be got to the bottom of. I will look in at the admin offices tomorrow and see what is holding up the money.'

Due to Hajime's efforts, the fellowship was processed within two weeks and the money released along with my book grant. There was also a 'settling advance'. I was puzzled and asked Hajime whether it could be a mistake. 'You are the only person I know who questions getting more money! If you must know, this is the university's way of saying sorry for the delay. I had told them how you had to survive on breadcrumbs and sleep with all your clothes on during this frigid spring because of the money being held up, and what a loss of face it would be for the venerable Kyodai if it ever came out.'

'I don't know how to thank you, Hajime. Could I buy you lunch, now that I can afford something more than breadcrumbs?'

'In fact, you can do better and have dinner with me instead. I will count that as a show of gratitude. First instalment, of course.'

That weekend, Hajime helped me choose a bike and we rode along the Kamo before going to one of the restaurants on its banks for dinner. I wasn't sure whether my leggings and pullover were suitable for the elegant restaurant he had selected.

'You are clad in beauty, which is always the best attire. Your hair can do with combing though.' I laughed and, pulling off the cotton hairband, ran my fingers through my loosened hair. Hajime lightly touched the hair falling around my face. 'This is better. Perfect, in fact.'

After we ordered food – miso soup and grilled tofu, fish and cold pickles, and spring greens – Hajime looked at me.

'So. How is he and what does he do?'

'Who?'

'Your boyfriend or fiancé in India, who is waiting for you to return.'

'There is no one.'

'You surprise me again. They let you escape?'

'Not without a struggle. And you? Someone in New York or elsewhere waiting for you?'

'She was here until a few months ago. Then she decided Kyoto was too provincial for her, crowded, not enough happening, whatever ... Imagine someone who has spent her entire life in New York City complaining about crowds! Anyway, she went back. Said she would wait for my contract to end, for me to choose between her and Kyoto.'

'And? When does your contract end?'

'In a week's time. But it was never a real choice in any case.' My stomach sank. 'How can I leave Kyoto? Kyoto is like a captivating, elegant woman, isn't she? Besides, I have just met you.'

'What does meeting me have to do with the captivating beauty of Kyoto holding you back?'

'Meeting an interesting woman in a beautiful city is the second best thing that could happen to anyone!'

'And what's the best thing?'

'All in good time!' he laughed as the waiter brought our food. 'Besides, your phone's ringing.'

It was Yuri. 'Father passed away, Meenu-chan ... It was terrible, this whole day, at the end...'

'Oh God ... Are you at the hospital? I'll come right away.'

Hajime was looking at me. 'What happened, Meena? Are you all right?'

'That was Yuri, Hajime. Her father died ... I need to get to the Kyoto Prefecture Hospital immediately. She's all by herself.'

'Sure. I will take you there.'

'No, please. I'm ruining your dinner.'

'You must eat something before we leave. You must have strength to help your friend. She is a friend, right?'

I nodded. I hadn't mentioned Yuri to Hajime.

YURI WAS IN the administrative section of the hospital. She was sitting at a small table, her eyes swollen, shivering in her cardigan. There were hospital forms spread on the table before her.

'Yuri,' I said.

She rose like a wave and wrapped her arms around me. 'Meenu-chan, Meenu-chan...' she sobbed, clinging to me.

A woman in a hospital uniform came up to us. 'Are you with them?' she asked Hajime in Japanese. Hajime bowed.

'The paperwork needs to be completed now, we are ready to release the body.'

'Do you think your friend can give the information required for filling these forms, Meena? These are necessary unfortunately.'

I silently helped Yuri to a chair and Hajime fetched cups of water from the dispenser. Yuri bowed to Hajime, sipped from the cup, and haltingly answered his questions as he filled the forms. It was past midnight by the time the formalities were completed, the body released and placed in the mortuary for removal next morning. Hajime insisted on dropping us home.

In the taxi, he asked me, 'Funeral arrangements will need to be made. Do you have any thoughts? Is there family?'

Yuri was leaning against me, her head on my shoulder, hands clutching mine. She said softly, 'I arranged for a funeral director last week. I knew the end was near ... My aunt arrives from Nara tomorrow...' She broke off, sobbing suddenly.

The taxi stopped at our apartment building.

'I thank you deeply for helping Meena and me, Hajime-san. Please accept my apologies for this inconvenience to you.'

'Not at all. I couldn't have let Meena go by herself. She loses her way, even on campus.' Yuri smiled faintly and put her arm around me. 'Please let me know if I can be of any help. I will see you at Uni, Meena. I will keep your bike safe until then.'

I looked at Hajime. I had been mostly silent since we had reached the hospital. He smiled, leaned and kissed me lightly on the cheek as I stood encircled by Yuri's arm.

I switched on the lights in the flat and pried off my sandals. Yuri sat on the chair in the tiny entrance and fumbled with the laces of her street shoes. I padded to the kitchen and warmed some milk, stirring crushed cinnamon, cardamom and turmeric into it, sweetening it lightly with cane sugar. I carried the glasses of milk to the living area. Yuri had given up trying to take off her shoes and was sitting with her arms wrapped around her shoulders. I set the glasses on the table and knelt by her side, undid the laces of her shoes and pulled them off, one by one. I made her drink the milk, helped her undress and slip on her nightshirt. She was limp and pliant as I tucked the comforter around her. I gently smoothed her hair. She lay on her back on the twin bed and looked up at me. She reached for my hands, her own shaking.

'Who is he, Meenu-chan? He, he...' her throat filled.

'He is an associate professor at the ICRS, Yuri. He helped me these past few weeks ... Without his help, my grant would not have come through. Now try to sleep, please. You have a lot to do tomorrow.'

I turned the lights out.

THE FUNERAL WAS a complicated affair. But for the funeral director and his team of nimble assistants, we would never have managed the ceremony. They brought the body to the apartment in a casket surrounded by flowers. Yuri, her aunt and I placed wreaths of white chrysanthemums and lilies on it. A Zen priest burned incense and recited the death sutras. Yuri's aunt prayed silently. I stood with my palms joined, my mind wandering. Unconnected images of my home, dark in the festive neighbourhood, the bike ride with Hajime, and long hospital corridors passed before me. When the prayers were over, the casket was carried to the crematorium in a shiny black van. Besides Yuri, her aunt and me, the only other mourners were two high-school graduates who worked at the ryokan in Nara. The cremation itself took a surprisingly short time. The ashes were placed in an urn by the assistant at the crematorium and handed over to Yuri.

Afterwards, the two youngsters left to see their families in Kyoto, and the funeral director escorted us back to our apartment. A catering service had delivered some food and cakes, a kind of Japanese high tea, and the four of us ate in silence. After the funeral director left, Yuri's aunt spoke about the tangled matters at the ryokan which she had been managing while Yuri's father, her brother-in-law, was ill. The account books needed to be updated – she hadn't been able to find the time to do so in the past three months. Her patience with the clumsy boys and girls Yuri's father employed was worn thin – they could never remember which linen was for which room, or which flower arrangements suited the various scrolls. She doubted whether she could carry on much longer, and wanted to return home to Kobe. Her husband's ashes were buried in the family grave there, and her son was in nearby Osaka. In short, Yuri needed to take the ryokan off her hands as soon as she could.

Two days after the funeral, Yuri left for Nara with her aunt. 'I wish you were coming with me, Meenu. But you can't, can you? You have your research schedule to keep...' Yuri's voice was tentative.

'I will try, Yuri. Perhaps in a few weeks or so, if you stay that long?'

Yuri's aunt looked alarmed. 'Yuri must stay in Nara at least until autumn,' she said. 'There are confirmed bookings until then.' And though she herself was not certain when the last guest would arrive or leave, she was certain that Yuri's father would not have wanted to throw off confirmed guests.

The dead must always be obeyed, I understood that. Irrespective of the love they received or gave while alive, unquestioning devotion to their real or imagined wishes must be observed after death.

Yuri gave me a kiss, 'Look after yourself, Meenu-chan.'

I GOT READY for university after Yuri left. Though it was spring, the wind was cold, sharper than in Tokyo. I put on a pair of jeans and a thick black pullover and chose an old silk dupatta, deep pink with tiny green, yellow and white tie-dye dots all over it, to wrap around my neck.

Hajime had not called or visited since that night at the hospital. I had informed my research director about the situation and that I needed a few days off, but hadn't emailed or messaged Hajime. I wondered what he made of Yuri and me.

I tried to think of Yuri as I rode on the train. She disliked Nara, it was the first home without her mother, a symbol of her mother's absence. But it was Hajime my thoughts circled around. I got off at Demachiyanagi station and walked towards the Yoshida campus. As I got closer to the university, my pace slackened until I came to a standstill at the big junction before the campus. The pedestrian crossing sign turned from red to green and back to red. I turned towards the Kamo river, a short ten-minute walk away.

It was the last week of March. The cherry blossoms were late this year and the trees along the Kamo were just beginning to bloom. The sparse blossoms were like white silk tassels. I watched the housewives with babies in prams and old people sitting or promenading along the riverside. There were groups of students running, doing calisthenics, cycling. Towards noon, I found a bench away from the crowds and opened my lunch box. Not inclined to cook that morning, I had packed the leftovers from last evening's meal.

'You don't want to eat that, it hardly looks appetizing.' Hajime was suddenly standing by my side. I stared mutely. 'When you didn't show up at Uni today, I had an idea you might be here. Why did you not come, Meena? Am I to bike-sit for you until you remember it ... and me?'

I was still wordless with surprise. He sat down by my side and said gently, 'I am sorry. My fault for not realizing that you must have been affected by the events of the past few days. Did you know him well?'

I had seen Yuri's father a few times at the hospital. His eyes seemed to be turned inwards, he could not take anything in, and the hand in which Yuri had placed mine had seemed already dead, it was so cold.

Hajime put his arm around me. 'Death's bewildering. It is always a jolt when viewed up close, the way it erases things which seemed so permanent and yet leaves other things behind. But we must live with death. The sakura bloom and wither, but their short season of beauty is something, isn't it?'

The afternoon sun was warm. The free ends of my dupatta caught in the spring breeze and whipped against Hajime's chest. I rested my head against his shoulder and closed my eyes.

YURI WAS STRUGGLING to put things in order in Nara. It appeared unlikely that she would be back before May.

She called frequently. 'Come to Nara for a weekend, Meenu,' she said. 'You will enjoy it. I go to bed alone and wake up alone ... I miss seeing you first thing in the morning. I miss you.'

I told her I would try, but my first review was coming up and work was piling.

I MET HAJIME almost every day. We rode around the streets of Kyoto on our bicycles and ate at out-of-the-way restaurants. We talked about the university, the books we read, politics, music. He was curious about India, and together we drew up travel itineraries.

My project review was scheduled for the second week of April, and I was worried. I had chosen to explore the position of women as reflected in Vedic literature and compare it with women characters in classical Japanese writings – mainly because the professor at Kyodai was an authority on Vedic Sanskrit and ancient Sanskrit texts. My own knowledge of Vedic Sanskrit and the classical Japanese script was limited and I was struggling.

Hajime spent hours prepping me on my work programme and reference texts from my notes and outlines. 'Relax,' he would say, as I fought back sudden tears. 'The first review is not a test, just an assessment that the work is on the right track. You know this. You will be fine.'

On the day of the assessment, I was physically sick, unable to eat any breakfast, nausea building inside me in waves. Throwing protocol to the winds – he was faculty in another stream and I a mere fellowship scholar – Hajime sat outside my research director's office during the review, reading *Dream of the Red Chamber* in kanji script. When I came out, he folded me in a hug. My eyes filled with tears, my breath caught. He kissed me on the forehead.

'Nothing less than a six-course meal at one of the exclusive places on Shoji-dori after the ordeal you've put me through over a first review! No, wait, I have a better idea – Shojin Ryori at Tenryuji tomorrow!'

'The vegetarian meal at the temple?'

'Yes. Dress modestly and practically.'

I smiled. 'I have heard the food's excellent.'

'Yes, the monks obviously know how to enjoy the illusions of life while they last. And now I must go look to the unfortunates, the development of whose literary understanding I am responsible for, and of which responsibility I have been extremely neglectful this whole morning.'

LATER THAT WEEK, we rode out to Arashiyama through the suburbs of Kyoto and up Mount Osore. The spring afternoon was as close to perfection as possible. Cherries were blooming everywhere now, and every breeze brought with it loose petals and subtle fragrances. The Zen gardens and tree-lined walks of Tenryuji were filled with golden April light.

We leaned our bikes against a wooden fence and walked to the restaurant in the temple complex. It was a low building with a corridor running along its length, a pond with koi fish on one side and eating rooms on the other. In the wood-tiled foyer, we exchanged our shoes for soft cloth slippers and followed the woman attendant down the corridor. She slid open a shoji door and showed us into a long room with tatami mats on the floor. Besides us, there was a group of three women seated at the extreme end of the long room. We sat on the floor, facing the door. I tucked my feet under me and watched Hajime struggle to find a comfortable position.

'It seems I'm more Japanese than you,' I laughed.

'Everyone's more Japanese than me. I am a fucking ugly American,' he said, crossing his legs uncomfortably. I looked at him in surprise. 'Sorry, Meena, that came out wrong. This betwixt-and-between existence of mine sometimes gets to me. I am as much an outsider here as I was back in US. In fact, more. There, only I knew I did not belong, others forgot it. Here, everyone remembers. It can get exhausting to be held at arm's length always.'

Two women entered, carrying lacquer trays laden with food, pots of tea and ceramic cups. They placed the trays in front of us, bowed and welcomed us to our meal with an elegant gesture of the hands. There were perfectly served portions of food in covered bowls and small saucers.

I selected a pair of chopsticks from the cutlery in the tray and removed the covers.

'Here's more proof – they have set forks, spoons and knives in my tray too. They never include silverware in trays served to Japanese customers.'

'You mind it so much, Hajime?'

'I grew up being told I am Japanese, Meena. Whenever I tried to be like others, I was reminded I was different. Eventually, I accepted it. I studied Japanese and Chinese along with modern literature and applied for teaching assignments in Asia. It was an absolute relief when I first came here. Everyone looked like me – the people on the trains, in shops, on the street. I was so thrilled, I used to smile at everyone, would try to strike up conversations. They all smiled politely, bowed and immediately retreated. I tried too hard, I think. I threw myself into what I thought was Japan – Buddhist temples, Shinto, Kabuki. But I remained a tourist, the odd person who always sat in the wrong place at formal dinners and had to learn the etiquette of Hanami by watching YouTube videos.' Hajime paused, picked up a clay dispenser and poured a small amount of rice vinegar on my cold tofu. 'Now eat that. The vinegar adds an acidic tang.'

'Hajime...' I began.

'First the cold, then the hot – that's the rule. And those funny green strands of seaweed are good but a bit salty.'

I ate in silence, but my thoughts hovered around what he had said. I knew his father taught at Princeton University and his mother was a students' counsellor at an elite private school. That he had graduated from Columbia before going on to Oxford for a degree in world literatures in English. The pictures tacked on his office wall were of walks in Yosemite, fishing in lonely, silvery streams, Thanksgiving dinners. They did not reconcile with the Hajime who wanted to be Japanese. I poured some green tea in my rice bowl and ate absently.

'Now that is very Japanese. I can't stand tea in rice. It is like eating waffles with soy sauce.'

I laughed. 'I like the soothing blandness.'

'I pray only in food though – I have no hope if it is blandness you like.'

'I like the way you pay yourself compliments.'

'I waited a long time for you to!'

After our meal, we walked in the temple grounds, empty of visitors in the middle of the week. Hajime led the way up a gently rising path. Invisible birds sang in trees. There was a viewing point, screened by pines and firs where the path ended. A wooden fence girded it and there was a stone bench in the green shade.

'This is quite special. Come here and look,' Hajime said.

I went up to him. Beyond the thickly clustered trees, there was a steep drop to the foot of the mountain, where a river – green, foaming, glowing – flowed. I was mesmerized.

'My God. It's like a painting. Jade river, blue mountains and the filigreed shade of trees in every tint of green. It's enough to make anyone lose their head.'

'Yes, it is like a real dream.'

Hajime put his arm around me and drew me closer. A warmth flooded me, my whole body responded to his touch, my arms wound tightly around him, fingers and hands touching him hungrily. His mouth sought mine, his hands were under my shirt, on my bare skin. Sensations swept through me.

'Meenu,' he murmured, 'Meenu.'

Yuri rose in my closed eyes, the way she was the night her father passed away – white, trembling, her cold fingers reaching for me. I couldn't bear it.

'Please, Hajime...' I struggled to pull away.

Hajime's face was flushed, his eyes flickered, 'Why, Meena? What happened? You want me, I can feel that. What is it?'

He turned my averted face until our eyes met.

'There's Yuri,' I stammered. 'She needs me.'

Hajime stared. 'That girl, your friend?'

'She and I ... We've been together the last few years.'

He let go of me slowly and walked to the stone bench.

'What have you been doing to me, Meena?' he said after too long. 'And to yourself? Why pretend to be someone else? What need could be greater than the need to be one's own self?'

He sat with his head in his hands. I couldn't hear the birds any more, the breeze from the river was chilly and my skin prickled. Hajime groaned, and the gravelly earth under his feet made a sound like a sigh. I looked at his hands, white in his dark, untidy hair. Sunlight filtering through the branches made a bright pattern on his bowed shoulders. I went to him and held his head against my breast, stroking his hair, his face.

He looked up. 'You are confusing me, Meena. I don't handle confusion well.'

'Neither do I,' I said, my eyes dropping. 'But it is clearing up now, I think.'

He pulled me on to his lap, holding me tight, kissing my cheek, ears, neck, as the birds began singing again.

That evening, Hajime and I walked by the Kamo under the blooming cherries. I told him about Tokyo, the neighbour's son, my mother. Before I knew it, I was telling him about the isolation, the deep loneliness, the unrelieved despair. He held my hand, kept pace with me and listened. I talked for hours. It was dark and a silver-foil moon was floating right in the middle of the Kamo, the koi fish and cherry-blossom petals shining bright, when I finally ran out of words. Hajime hailed a taxi and took me to his flat in Kitayama.

That night, as he held me and entered me, I felt the relief that had eluded me all this while.

In the morning, I woke up to find Hajime's tall body curled around me. Like me, he slept on his left side too.

ALL THROUGH APRIL and May, Hajime and I spent all our free time together.

I stayed over at his flat frequently, keeping a change of clothes, my toothbrush and my kajal in the satchel I carried around with me. He seldom came to the flat Yuri and I occupied together – the twin beds were not comfortable to sleep in, and he was not fond of the simple rice-and-vegetable dinners I cooked. He, on the other hand, had an elaborate kitchen in his flat and carefully prepared sukiyaki, miso and bean curd, fried rice and fresh sushi for our meals. When he discovered my partiality towards Italian food, he bought a large, expensive aluminium-plated pan from Daimaru and cooked pasta, making the sauce from scratch.

Yuri called from time to time. Her aunt had left, and she was managing the ryokan while scouting for a buyer to take it over. My conversations with her were always hurried – there was either work or Hajime waiting.

One evening, towards the end of May, I came home briefly to change. Hajime had booked a Kabuki performance for later that night. I entered the flat and was startled to find Yuri on the sofa in the living room, reading, a cup to of tea on the table by her side.

She smiled. 'Meenu-chan,' she said softly. 'I have been waiting.'

'Yuri! God, you surprised me. I had no idea...'

'You've been busy the last few days, Meenu-chan. I was

worried about you.' Her eyes rested on me tenderly. 'I missed you very much.'

I looked at my watch. I had to hurry if I were to make it to the Kabuki performance in time. I dropped my satchel on the sofa and gave Yuri a hug.

'I wish you had told me. I wouldn't have agreed to go to the Kabuki this evening with friends.' I spoke as normally as I could.

Yuri looked at me. 'Of course, you must not disarrange your plans. The tickets must have been bought and they are expensive. Do you need to leave right away?'

'Yes. Well, almost. I must change first. So sorry, Yuri.' I squeezed her shoulder and rushed to the bedroom.

Yuri was sipping her tea when I stepped out in a peacock-blue silk dress, the one I had bought in Tokyo for a formal dinner at the university. I wore the pearl and crystal earrings Hajime had gifted me. 'You look beautiful, Meenu-chan,' she said. 'And different.'

'Must be the earrings,' I laughed. 'They are new. I need to hurry. You're not going back tonight, are you? I should be back around ten thirty or eleven.' I waved to her and dashed out.

Hajime was waiting for me at the theatre. 'You make watching Kabuki an adventure. We are dangerously close to missing the first act – the fun one with the shapeshifting fox and the general's wife and moving cherry trees.' He wrapped his arm around my waist as we joined the few latecomers up the ornate staircase of the theatre to our balcony seats.

'I'm sorry, Hajime. Yuri's returned suddenly. I had to say I was going to the theatre with friends from Uni. I feel bad about leaving her alone. She's back after so long...'

We settled into our seats and Hajime handed me the programme. 'Did I mention? You look stunning. You own this blue.' He kissed me. 'You did absolutely the right thing, Meena. I don't see why you should feel bad. Now be here and watch.'

The beautiful velvet curtain rose in great loops, revealing the musicians and singers, the stage set for the first act.

After the fourth act, instead of lingering in the theatre cafeteria, talking over the performance, prolonging the magic of the show, we left. I was in a hurry, Yuri was waiting. Hajime walked me to the station in silence. He held my hand the whole time, as we waited for my train.

The apartment was dark and empty when I reached. There was a sheet of paper, weighed down with a beautifully wrapped manju cake, by my bedside table.

> My Meenu-chan. Hope you enjoyed Kabuki. I am taking the last bus back to Nara. I came to see a buyer. He is interested and would like to see the ryokan at the earliest. If all goes well, I might be able to conclude everything in the next few weeks.

There was a postscript:

> You looked like I have never seen you before. I longed to take you in my arms ... Your toothbrush fell out of your satchel. You carry underwear, clothes in your bag ... I wonder why?

My heart beat fast. I felt annoyed that I hadn't been more careful and placed the bag in my closet where it belonged, and that Yuri had noticed.

I told Hajime about it as we shopped at a supermarket in his neighbourhood for our dinner one evening. Hajime continued looking at the cheeses. 'Shall we have Emmental or Gruyère?' We walked back to his flat. Hajime unlocked the door and turned to me. 'You know, you need to decide, Meena. Whether you want to go on pretending until every bit of you is lost. It's not you whom Yuri needs. Surely you realize that?'

He handed me the key, and taking the bag of Roma tomatoes and olives from my hands, went to the kitchen, leaving me at the entrance.

YURI RETURNED TOWARDS the end of June. She had managed to sell the ryokan to the buyer from Kyoto. She was not due back at Tokyo University until fall and began looking for a job. She was the same as always towards me – gentle, loving. But a sadness lay in her eyes, in her smile.

With her return and my second review approaching, Hajime and I met less often, I could no longer stay over at his flat. Hajime did not complain, but at times he would look at me, an unsettling brooding look in his eyes, and would hold me tight before I caught the train back to my apartment.

Yuri found a job with a publishing company that specialized in pamphlets, commemorative books and monographs on places of interest in Kyoto prefecture. Its offices were in North Kyoto, on the other side from Kyodai.

I mentioned this to Hajime. 'It makes me feel much more comfortable that Yuri works far from the Yoshida campus,' I said.

Hajime looked at me for a moment. 'Why does it make you feel comfortable, Meena? What would happen if she began working around here or even enrolled at Kyodai? You wouldn't see me at all? Tell me, Meena,' he said quietly. 'Do you let her touch you? Do you sleep with her?'

The first night Yuri was back, she had come into my bed. I had stiffened as her fingers had touched my neck, my back, like falling leaves, and her breath had stirred my hair. I had lain still, pretending to be asleep, ignoring her endearments.

'Don't be so crude, Hajime, please. Don't say these things, they hurt...'

'Why not? All this dishonesty is crude, hurtful. I want to know if she has you while I lie alone thinking of you. What do you think you are doing, Meena? Where are you? Do you think we can continue like this indefinitely?'

I felt tears welling in my eyes.

Hajime reached across the table and took my hand. 'Why is this so difficult, Meena? I thought you had solved it. You know now, don't you?'

I nodded. But I needed some time, Yuri needed some time.

I CHECKED MY phone. *I am waiting*, Hajime had texted.

'You carry on with the insurance stuff, Yuri, it's important. I have things to complete at Uni. The last few weeks, I was swamped with the review preparations. I must get on with the work programme for the coming quarter.'

I went into the bedroom and, opening the closet, pulled out a sleeveless dress of blue voile. The end of the dress caught at something in the closet. I yanked at it in my hurry. The contents of the shelf just below clattered to the floor – a box of beaded chokers and bangles I no longer wore, my satchel, a folder of documents.

Yuri came in. 'Hasty as ever, my Meenu-chan,' she smiled and bent down to pick up the fallen articles.

I gathered the beads and, putting them back in the box, said, 'What do you think I should do with these, Yuri? They are pretty enough, but I don't wear them any more. And this bangle is cracked.'

I turned. Yuri was holding a sheet of paper. One of Hajime's emails that I had printed, a verse he had written for me. *To my darling,* it began. *Hold me/ as you did that first time/ blood sang in my ears/ breath fell like petals/ touched to the quick/ you called my name/ My name in your voice/ is the sound of blood-red petals/ raining on us.*

'Why would Hajime-san write this to you, Meenu-chan?'

I remained silent.

'You've been seeing him? You've been with him? Why would you bring this into our togetherness, Meenu-chan? We created this, and it came so dear. We both gave up so much for it – my memories, your family ... To throw it away for him, for a man...' She let the paper fall from her hand and leaned against the wall. 'I don't understand this ... A man who could have any other woman, but he must take you from me. Why would you exchange real love for a man's desire? Tell me why, Meenu-chan? First my mother, and now you...'

I was stung. 'I'm not your mother, Yuri. I am breaking no vows and I have tried to remain. Honestly, I have. But Hajime ... he moves me in ways you don't ... I can't help it, can't help being myself.'

Yuri looked at me with baffled, unbearable eyes.

'I must go now, Yuri. But I will come back. I ... we shall talk. You'll see, you'll understand...' I could not look at her any longer. 'Both of us have to accept this.'

Yuri remained silent, but her eyes never left me as I picked up my satchel and bicycle keys and walked to the door.

I cycled away with all my strength until my lungs burnt. Tears rained down my cheeks, blinding me, and I stopped at a water fountain to bathe my face, my neck. I reached Hajime's flat, sweaty and tear-stained, my shirt damp. He opened the door at the first ring of the doorbell, took one look at me, and held me to himself.

He spoke softly, his mouth near my ear. 'I am sorry this is tough on you, but this was bound to happen, Meena.' He stroked my hair. 'You want this, don't you?'

'Yes, I do. And this is right, you and I, we are right ... But I have been ignorant, Hajime, very ignorant. And now, Yuri is hurt...'

Hajime led me to the bathroom. He turned on the tap to fill the large bathtub, dropped handfuls of bathing salts in it, and poured a whole vial of bath oil. He took my crumpled shirt and linen trousers off, dried the sweat on my body with a small towel, and gently lowered me into the bath. I lay back in the warm water while he peeled off his clothes and came to me. He cradled me against him, running his hands all over my body, soaping me, pouring water on me with his cupped palms. I closed my eyes and felt the stiff knots open, the twists unravel. There was peace.

LATER THAT EVENING, I left Hajime's apartment. 'I must speak to Yuri, try to make her understand. I can't leave in anger and misunderstanding after all this while,' I told him. 'Besides, I need clothes. I will pack my things and be back in a couple of hours.'

Hajime was reluctant. 'Rest today, Meena, you are tired. Go tomorrow.'

'I'm not tired any longer, and if I am when I return, I'd really enjoy another bath.'

I kissed him.

The flat was dark when I entered. Perhaps Yuri had gone out. I switched on the lights. The small living and dining area was tidy, the table by the window neatly arranged. I stepped into the bedroom and opened my closet. It was tidy too. Yuri must have put things in order after I left.

I decided to pack some essentials and return the next day to talk to her. I pulled down the suitcase from the top shelf and, taking my clothes from the hangers, folded them into it. I entered the bathroom to get my night cream and washcloth.

That's when I saw her. She was sitting propped up against the bathtub, her face white, her unseeing eyes fixed on the place where I stood, just inside the door. Her arm was trailing in the tub in a pool of drying blood.

I reached down and touched her cold foot. My body shook uncontrollably and I could not breathe. I pulled out my phone and managed to dial Hajime's number.

'We have killed her, you and I,' I tried to say, but I could only gasp. My voice had dried up like Yuri's blood.

PRAKASH

'ALL THIS ... It hasn't been easy, has it?' Prakash said. 'Things haven't turned out easy.'

Leela raised her head. She was slicing kachri. The room was filled with its ripe smell. Munnaji lay on his side on the large bed by the wall, among carefully arranged bolster pillows to ease his back. His eyes were closed, and he snored softly, intermittently. Prakash's eyes moved from Munnaji to the drawings that hung on the wall beside his bed. Detailed and precise, they were done to scale in coloured drafting pencils. They were the front, back and cross-section views of a collar necklace, one of Haruko's project pieces. Some were drawn by Haruko and others by Leela. After Munnaji's accident, Leela had pasted the thick foreign paper on to pieces of cardboard and hung the drawings where he could see them.

Leela looked at her father's inert frame. Yes, it hadn't been easy, the past few years. Perhaps it wouldn't be easy in the future either. 'Everything changed the year after Haruko Jiji left. Dadi-sa died and then Pappaji almost died in the accident.' Leela glanced at her father. His eyes were closed.

She held her breath for a second to listen to the faint rustle of his breathing. 'Everyone wondered how he survived, there was so much blood on the road in the bazaar. But it is better now. Everything's getting better.'

Prakash too looked at Munnaji. 'Well, it is what it is. Brainstem injuries are tough. At least there are no other complications. I must say, he is being looked after very well. It's almost five years since he's been bedridden, isn't it? And not a single bedsore or any atrophy of the limbs. His complexion is good too and there seems to be no breathing discomfort. You have a nurse for him?'

'No, Amma and I do everything. It is not difficult, he is like a baby now. Amma even calls him Munna sometimes and sings him lullabies.' Leela laughed. 'You saw last time when you were here, how she was massaging his legs? She rubs and massages him all over, every day. Only these few days she is busy with Badi Jiji.'

'Your sister has delivered?'

'Yes, the baby came two weeks ago. Amma can't think straight right now, she is that happy! Badi Jiji's first delivery, and that too a boy! She is busy doing something or the other for the baby all day and most of the night too. She has no time for anyone else, not even for Pappaji.'

'Of course. And that's why you are home, to look after Munnaji? Your mother told me last time that you work at the family gaddi now.'

'Yes. But I have not stopped working, I have five pieces to complete before the end of the month. So, I work here in the afternoons.' She pointed to the small wooden work desk in one corner of the room. 'And Pappaji likes to watch me while I work. If he is awake, his eyes remain fixed on me the whole time. No one believes me, but I think he understands everything. I know by the look in his eyes if I make an error in the kundan setting, or if the enamel work is flawed. Haruko Jiji says this is what people do in foreign – work from home, she calls it. You remember she used to work here too when she broke her leg? This is her desk.' Prakash nodded slightly and glanced at the wooden desk. 'You know I work with Haruko Jiji, Doctor Saab?'

'Yes, your mother told me.'

'She is famous now, Doctor Saab. She has a big shop in Singapore, but she says she learnt the most here. She still uses the words of jewellery craft from here – jadav, katav, taraash, nageena, kundan...' Leela smiled. 'Now that I work at our gaddi, the biradari calls me names. They were all right when I used to help Kako-sa and do ordinary bazaar-work for him. But now when I do real fine work and we have money, they are swarming around like angry red ants. A girl can't have her own gaddi, they say.' She paused and looked at Prakash. 'It is strange no, Doctor Saab? Haruko Jiji left and everything changed, and now because of her, things are changing again. It is like one of those stories Dadi-sa used to tell – the princess left and the saffron garden dried up, and when she returned the flowers bloomed again.'

Prakash glanced at the drawings on the wall. 'Her being here was strange in the first place. I remember everyone at the hospital was surprised when your father brought her to the casualty ward. You don't often see a Japanese girl in a government hospital in Jaipur. She was in bad shape too. They were very bad, very painful fractures – her leg was broken in two places.'

'She never once complained about the pain though. And she taught me while she was recovering. I would go from gaddi to gaddi in the lanes, clicking pictures of old ornaments with her phone, and she would sit up in bed and teach me the techniques of design drawing. For hours she would sit, making detailed drawings of old timanyas and bangadis and sheeshphools.'

'What a lot you remember! You used to be with her all the time when she was here.'

'Yes! Badi Jiji used to tease me, she used to call me Haruko's tail. Wherever Haruko goes, the tail faithfully follows, she used to say. And do you remember when you came to the haveli the first time to check her leg? You couldn't believe that she was learning jewellery craft here, in the lanes of Johri Bazaar ... *But, but you studied at the university in New York!*' Leela mimicked the doctor's deep voice.

Prakash smiled. 'What a lot you remember,' he repeated.

'I remember everything. The days you used to come and chat and drink tea with us, and tell us about the hospital, about accidents and operations, those were the best days. Do you know that Haruko Jiji used to call you the real deal? She used to say you were a real doctor, someone who worked to ease pain. But then you stopped visiting.' Leela sliced the last piece of the yellow-skinned, fragrant kachri, wiped her hands on a faded cotton hand towel and picked up a sharp green chilli. 'Amma said you must have gotten busy with preparations for your wedding. Your marriage was fixed around Teej that year, no? You didn't invite us.' She looked at him from the corner of her eye. 'You forgot us no, Doctor Saab? Perhaps you didn't want us to come to your wedding.' She smiled, her eyes on the chilli she was slicing. 'Haruko Jiji couldn't have come in any case. She left before Teej, soon after the rains began that year.'

Prakash moved in his chair. 'This is the same room, isn't it? She stayed here too when she was recovering...'

'Yes, Pappaji brought her here from the hospital, this was the most convenient room. All other rooms are either inside the courtyard or upstairs, and you had said she shouldn't walk. And it is never boring in here – you can look out into the lane without being seen. Only Dadi-sa didn't like Jiji's staying in this room. She used to say it was wrong for a girl to sleep in the men's baithak. It brings bad luck, she used to say.' Leela cast a fleeting look at him. 'But all this is old stuff. You tell me about yourself, Doctor Saab. How have you been all these years? You must have children now. Does your wife still like Tokyo? I remember she liked it so well there that she did not want to return to Jaipur.'

Prakash placed his empty teacup on the wooden stool. 'My wife has never been to Tokyo.' Leela looked up, astonished. 'Meena ... my fiancée ... she and I, we did not get married ... She did not return that time.'

Leela rested the knife in the dish of sliced vegetables. 'She didn't return? Then what happened? Why did you stop coming suddenly? You liked her no, Doctor Saab? I know you liked Haruko Jiji.'

'It was all very long ago, Leela. More than five years ago. You were a child then...'

'I was almost fourteen. I had eyes enough to see. Haruko Jiji didn't say anything after you suddenly stopped coming, but I know she waited. Do you know she went to the hospital? I went along with her too, but you were not there. Some other doctor cut the plaster off her leg. When we walked out, she held my hand but she wouldn't look at me. Afterwards, she told me she would leave soon. Dadi-sa said her heart was like a diya emitting smoke when she left Jaipur.'

'She always meant to leave, Leela, she used to say so all the time. From Jaipur to Bombay, Benares, Hyderabad ... To learn all there was to learn about jewellery making, that was her plan.'

'But she always meant to return, Doctor Saab. You laughed when she said she'd come back and set up her own place here. You didn't believe her, but she meant it. She told me there was no place like the bazaar for inspiration. *When I come back, Leela,* she used to say, *we'll have our own gaddi, you and I, and we will be the best sunars in the old jewellers' market.* But she has never returned, not even now when I do only her work at the gaddi.'

'And you think it is because of me that she hasn't come back...?'

Leela bent her head over the vegetables she was chopping. Soon after she had begun crafting jewellery for Haruko's boutique, a call had come one evening. She was at work in the shop her family had owned for five generations. It was Haruko. 'Guess what,' she had said. 'I am in Bombay this week. I have booked you a return ticket. Come over. Let's see the stuff you've done so far and work out how it fits in the line I am doing for this autumn.' Leela had jumped up from her desk. 'You are in India, Jiji? Come to Jaipur, come and see the bazaar and my work. Pappaji will be so happy to see you.' There was a pause before Haruko had replied, 'I have work here, Leela, perhaps next time. This time you come over.' 'You don't want to come to Jaipur,' Leela had challenged. 'I learnt everything I needed to learn there already, Leela.'

'Does she remember? Has she asked about me?'

Leela made a long, precise cut along the length of a green chilli and spilt its bitter, white seeds into a little bowl. She shook her head. No, Haruko had not asked about the doctor. It was she, Leela, who had mentioned him. She had told

Haruko that he was a well-known surgeon at the big hospital now, people spoke of him with respect. Haruko had listened in silence. She hadn't asked any questions, so there had been no need for Leela to tell her that Prakash hadn't visited them in years, that she didn't know how his bride had looked on their wedding day, how many children he had, whether he was happy.

When she had returned from the gaddi one evening a few weeks ago, and had found Prakash in the baithak, speaking quietly with her mother, her thoughts had flown to Haruko. Prakash had looked older, and his eyes behind the rimless glasses were shadowed. 'It's a coincidence that your tenant works for an orthopaedic implants company,' he had said to her mother. 'If he hadn't mentioned it, I would never have known about Munnaji's accident.' He had looked at Munnaji's old reports and pursed his lips. 'Perhaps some more tests to see what can be done,' he had said. 'Let me ask a neurosurgeon I know. He is very good, his advice could be useful. But why did you not contact me when all this happened?' Leela had it on the tip of her tongue to ask why he had not visited them again, why he had cut away, but she had kept quiet and made tea for him. Her mother had said once after Pappaji's accident, 'Surely Doctor Saab would know how to make your father well, should we go to him?' In the end, they hadn't. By that time, they knew Munnaji was well enough. So what if he couldn't move or speak clearly? He relished food and slept peacefully, and seemed calm and smiled too. That was enough. His being there was enough. Besides, their money had run out. So they had brought him back to the haveli and there he had remained. Now, when Prakash had appeared again, Leela had debated telling Haruko, but in the end decided not to. Things were all right as they were.

'Perhaps she has forgotten...'

Leela chopped the chillies into small pieces, releasing their tartness. She remembered the morning six years ago, the morning after the first rains had fallen and the path leading to the baithak had turned into slush. Haruko was still not permitted to walk much, and Leela had brought her sweet milk-porridge for breakfast. She had found her sitting up in bed, shivering, her clothes, bed sheet and coverlet all damp. The floor was covered in mud, and the snowy cast extending from her left foot to her knee had brown smudges on it. Leela had quietly fetched a cloth to wipe the floor. She had removed the bedspread and helped Haruko change. That day, though she had not asked and Haruko had not explained, Leela knew who had left those muddy footprints on the baithak floor. It was only when she visited Haruko in Bombay, when she saw her standing by the big glass window in the hotel room, looking out at the grey sea, her face obscured by the light that was streaming in, that Leela had asked the question. 'What had happened, Jiji? Doctor Saab came that night, didn't he?' Haruko had remained silent for so long that Leela wondered whether she had heard her. 'You always observed well, Leela,' she had said eventually. 'You were puzzled then too, and hurt for me. I saw that, but I could not comfort you. I was trying to resolve things for myself. Yes, he came that night and I want you to know that I am all right with what happened. He did not force me or anything. He just wasn't there enough, he was in distress. I thought he'd come out of it when he saw that I was real. I thought he'd begin feeling, finally – for real, and not because of a habit or a false memory. But of course I was wrong. Anyway, it was all for the best. I learnt never to let something like that sneak up on me and surprise me ever again. I learnt to be safe, always. I know now that the only lasting experience is capturing beauty in my work, all other kinds are just temporary.' When she finished, it was Haruko who had smiled and Leela who had tried to blink back her tears.

'I DID NOT expect her to remember ... Things didn't mean the same to her...'

Leela raised her eyes and looked directly at him. 'Is that what you tell yourself, Doctor Saab? This much even I understood at that time, that Haruko Jiji broke more than her leg, and I can also tell you that whatever was broken has not joined up straight.'

Prakash met her gaze. 'You blame me ... Does she blame me too?'

'Should she, Doctor Saab?' He looked away. 'I didn't ask then and Haruko Jiji never told me, but I saw how she waited day after day for you, in suspense.'

'You don't understand, Leela. It was not that simple ... She was from a different world, everything was different with her. Her mother was in a mental hospital, she hadn't seen her in years. When she was here among strangers, with a broken leg, her father was playing golf somewhere ... She had no family, no people of her own ... It wouldn't have worked.'

'If you knew this, if she was so different, why did you come to her that night? Her being from a different world did not stop you then.'

A fiery flush spread over the doctor's sensitive skin. 'Do you think I don't think about that night? That one night comes back to me all the time. I dream of it often, always the same dream. She is holding me in her arms, I can't quite see her face, but I know that if I look closely it won't be her, won't be Haruko but the other ... I know it would be Meena's face I will see ... and then I can't resist ... I try to look and suddenly she is gone. No one's there, no one's holding me. I begin to disappear too, tissues, muscles, bones, organs, glands. Everything vanishes bit by bit, like a bizarre anatomy demonstration. I feel piercing pain, but I can't cry out because I have no tongue, no diaphragm, no voice ... I lose everything in my dream ... again and again...' Despite the whirring fan, sweat stood out on the doctor's forehead and glistened on his neck. Leela got up and fetched a steel jug from a niche in the wall. She poured water in a glass and gave it to him. He sipped it slowly. 'That evening, Meena's sisters came to our home. Her parents could not bring themselves to face us, they could not look my father and mother in the eye and tell them that the daughter they had raised was living with a woman in Tokyo and did not want to come back. So her sisters came and told my sister. We couldn't understand at first ... she loved a woman ... How could she?'

Munnaji coughed. Phlegm rattled in his throat. Leela went to him and helped him spit in an earthen bowl. She held a child's drinking cup to his mouth and tilted it until drops of water trickled between his open lips. His eyes remained closed all through. She set the cup down on the wooden stool.

'So she was different too, Doctor Saab, no?'

'Leela, I knew her kind of differentness ... I had known it all my life. Her out-of-place bright clothes, her armful of bangles, her restlessness ... My mother used to say Meena is celebrating a festival none of us have any idea of. She would go about smiling brightly, unseeingly, never listening to what was said, answering questions no one asked...' Prakash shook his head, still surprised. 'Strange things interested her. Take Japan. Why did she have to go to Japan? None of us, no one we knew, no one we had heard of even, had gone to Japan. But she wanted to go. When her parents said they wouldn't let her, she was beside herself ... I remember she came rushing to our home – she was always rushing – her hair was damp with sweat and her kajal was smudged. She caught her dupatta in the door and tore it as she pulled at it. I ... I can never forget how she looked that day ... And the way she looked at me, it was like her glance was something shining and sharp, like a scalpel ... It sliced everything away. She spoke in gasps, *They won't let me go, don't you side with them, I'll never speak to you again.*' Prakash cleared his throat and drank some water. 'In the end she went. I knew that she would, that she'd find a way. While everyone was scolding her and telling her how it was unthinkable, she wrote to the university and accepted the fellowship, called up her advisor and explained the difficulty with her family and asked for help with air tickets. No one knew how to stop her. She'd done the same thing when she was at school too. She was a top ranker in the board exams. Everyone told her she should take science. I was in medical college. It would have been sensible for her to study medicine. On the last day for submitting admission forms, she handed her mother a letter and climbed into the school bus. She had already applied for admission in the arts section a week earlier, so there was no point shouting at her, she had written. She couldn't imagine seeing sick people every day of her life, and she hated the smell of hospitals.' Prakash unlaced his fingers and looked at his palms. 'Smell of a hospital ... As if that matters. There are so many other things about being a doctor, but she won't think of those or consider them. She was determined not to study medicine because she hated the smell of formaldehyde. Her parents were very angry, but what could they do?'

Leela sifted the lentils in a large steel platter and picked out bits of straw and tiny pebbles. Prakash watched her absently.

'She was baffling, even as a child. She'd never play our games. She'd pretend she lived elsewhere, was someone else. Once, she told all her friends that she went to London during the summer vacations. She described the streets of London, the guards outside Buckingham Palace, the red double-decker buses ... When everyone found out she was lying, the principal called her. She told him that she had read English novels during the vacations and didn't he himself say that world could be seen through books? She was punished in school and at home, but she stuck to her story.'

'She had imagination, Doctor Saab. Sometimes it is needed to make up for the lack of real things around us.'

'Perhaps. Whatever it was, it got her into trouble all the time.'

Leela rubbed the steel blade of the knife with a bit of lemon to get rid of the chilli's sharpness. 'Was she beautiful?'

Doctor looked at his hands again. 'I ... I suppose she was. My batchmates used to say she was a looker.' Prakash smiled faintly. 'She would never be still, she seemed always to flicker away when I looked at her. I used to think, someday I will hold her and she'll be still, I will look at her for as long as I wish, just look at her, make sure she's there ... In my dream I try to assure myself that it is her ... It is always Meena's face I look for, but she always recedes and everything falls apart.'

'If it was like that, Doctor Saab, if you loved her like that, then why did you come to Haruko Jiji? What was that about?'

Prakash cast his eyes around. Munnaji was still snoring softly, his face relaxed.

'What can I say? I can't explain. I was not thinking that night, I was trying not to think. Everything was in a whirl. I left home while Meena's sisters were still there. I just couldn't stand being there a moment longer, so I said I had night duty at the hospital. I drove around a bit, but it was claustrophobic in the car. I parked it somewhere in the bazaar and stepped out ... And then, somehow I was here, in front of the haveli. It was raining. I stood in the street for a while and then knocked. When Haruko opened the door and took me in, I ... I just wanted to tell her about Meena ... But I couldn't speak. Nothing seemed clear any longer... Then she held me and the confusion seemed to ease a bit...' He cleared his throat. 'But afterwards, when I left, it all came back. I was numb. But I couldn't lie in bed, unmoving, unseeing ... I had to get up every day, get dressed, see my parents, talk to friends. When it became unbearable, I moved to the hostel for senior residents, did round-the-clock duties, worked until I could barely stand upright.' Prakash emptied his glass. 'My parents would say I ought to get married, time was passing, it was awkward for them to explain what happened, why I wouldn't marry. In the end, I married one of my juniors. What else could I do?' He shrugged. 'They were right. I had completed my specialization and was offered a position in the hospital.

It was time to have a family.' Leela kept her eyes on the platter she held, her fingers moved among the lentils. 'And it all turned out okay. My wife's very calm, content. She is never restless, and she gets along well with my mother too. We have two daughters. It's a bit tough for her right now because both our daughters are young and she has a teaching appointment at a private medical college, but she manages. I think it's all okay.'

'Calm and content,' Leela repeated. 'And how about you, Doctor Saab? How about that dream? Have you told your wife about it?'

Prakash stared. The air in the room went still. In the ensuing silence, Leela heard the stray her mother fed every evening pattering at the entrance, its claws clicking on the stone slabs. The intense, unrelieved heat of early May had set in, and the hot winds from the desert blew over the city until late in the evening. It was turning out to be a wasted day. She hadn't had a chance to work on the piece she was crafting. Presently, she would go to the kitchen in the inner courtyard and cook the kachri with green chillies and fenugreek seeds, garnish the lentils and cook gruel with coriander seeds and herbs for Badi Jiji.

Eventually, Prakash spoke. 'You think that is the solution? To damage the undamaged?'

Leela gathered the siftings from the lentils into the palm of her hand and rose. 'I am only nineteen, Doctor Saab. What can I tell you about solutions? But I don't think losing everything or being safe are solutions. I don't think keeping losses to yourself can make anyone content. Pappaji used to say that if there is a flaw in the first moulding, however much you patch it up, the ornament will remain imbalanced. The only solution is to start over again, even though precious metal is lost in the process.' She stepped to the door and tossed the bits of straw and pebbles into the dirt patch.

'Some things cannot be remade or unmade. I wouldn't know where to start. Or how. Even if I wanted to. And this is okay ... It wouldn't have worked any other way...'

'You join bones and cure pain, no, Doctor Saab? You would know the answer yourself. Is ignoring pain a way to treat it too?' She switched on the electric light and joined her palms for a moment in prayer.

'I tried ... once,' Prakash said. 'I found out that she ... that Meena was back. She had written to her youngest sister. She was in Delhi, teaching at a university. That girl in Tokyo ... something had happened to her, she didn't say what. But she had left Japan for good, was never going back. Of course, she was not going to return to Jaipur either. Her sisters thought it was better that she stayed away.'

'Why?'

'It would have shamed her parents. They are still our neighbours. And the news about Meena and the girl in Tokyo had spread among relatives. Anyone can see that it would have been difficult all around if she returned. I understood that, but I just wanted to see her, even if only once ... So I wrote to her. I told her I wasn't angry or anything, I bore no grudges, just wanted to meet her.'

'And what did she say?'

'Initially, she refused. She said she couldn't see the point. Nothing's to be gained by meeting, she wrote, but in the end she agreed.'

'But why did you want to see her?'

'I ... I don't quite know ... I thought something would change if I met her ... That dream would change. Perhaps something could be salvaged from the loss...'

'And did anything change, Doctor Saab?'

The doctor avoided her eyes. 'No ... I didn't see her. I ... I waited at the place we were to meet, but she didn't come.'

Leela let out her breath and stooped to pick up the vessels. Sounds of evening meals being cooked floated in from the street, the clatter of rolling pins and pans, cumin and coriander crackling in hot oil, and rotis being slapped expertly on to iron griddles.

The doctor rose. 'It is quite late. Tell your mother I have sent Munnaji's reports to the neurosurgeon. I will come again once I hear from him.' Leela nodded. At the door, he paused. 'If ... if Haruko visits, will you tell me?'

Leela balanced the steel platter with lentils on the flat of her palm and met his gaze. 'No,' she said.

Prakash nodded slightly and stepped into the street outside.

HAJIME

THE ISLAND WAS a vivid picture in azure, emerald and ivory. A flight of brightly coloured parakeets made a racket in the wild guava trees, and salamanders with flashing colours scurried among leaves and pebbles. The wide and curving beach was dazzling under the brilliant sun, its white sands dotted with large clumps of broad-leaved, bright green weeds. The sea girding it, a deep blue with hints of green. It was an uncharacteristic June day, not a trace of monsoon clouds in the boundless blue sky.

Haruko flung a muscular arm out. 'Look at all this! I see a necklace – turquoise and aquamarine set in uneven waves, clusters of peridots, a shimmering white mother-of-pearl base, a necklace called Selingan!'

They had reached the island earlier that morning. After a quick shower, they had left their log chalet to explore. The salt in the sea breeze had begun crisping Hajime's hair, and his feet were dusted with the talcum-powder-white sand.

He pointed to the circular wire enclosures everywhere on the island. 'What could these be for?'

'They are to protect turtles' eggs from marauding lizards,' Haruko explained.

'From these tiny salamanders?'

'No, no. Not these aquamarine and amethyst beauties. I meant the monitors, large and hungry and ugly. You'll see, the place is teeming with them. They roam the paths and roost on verandas, bold as brass and a complete nuisance at times. You can walk right by them and they won't budge. They are a real menace here. They and the fishermen across the waters both like turtle eggs.'

Hajime had never seen a monitor lizard in real life, only on TV in nature documentaries, and was curious.

Haruko turned a brown leaf over with the toe of her sandal. A salamander, its tail brilliantly blue, flickered among the dry leaves. She looked at it intently as it scampered away. 'If I can capture this blue, no matter in which material, if I can create it with chemicals or enamel or stones, I will craft something great.' Haruko shielded her eyes with her palm. 'Even the sunlight here has blue highlights!' She pointed to a clump of bright green weeds. 'There's a monitor, and the biggest I have ever seen.'

Hajime looked. From among the green leaves, a long, dark neck rose a good foot or so above the ground, surmounted by a flat, triangular head. The rest of the lizard's body was hidden from view. It turned its sinuous neck.

'Look, it is staring at us,' Hajime said. He watched as the great lizard turned its head away and shifted, settling back among the weeds. 'It seems so disdainful of us, Haruko, I bet it thinks we are interlopers here, trespassers of a mere hundred thousand years' vintage, while it has ranged here since the beginning of time, ever since it climbed out of the ancient oceans and grew feet.'

Haruko didn't hear him. She had turned towards the sea, twining her long fingers, looking out at the brilliant waves.

HAJIME HAD MET Haruko almost a year ago in Singapore, on the Helix Bridge spanning Marina Bay. It was a typical Singapore evening, hot and humid. There were tourists taking pictures in the middle of the bridge, blocking it entirely. A group of young women were struggling to get the right angle with their phones clamped on to lightweight aluminium sticks. With their dark, arched brows and kohl-lined eyes, they had a superficial resemblance to Meena. He had stood on one side, unhurried, gazing at the group.

'Pretty. But too young for you, don't you think?' A woman with Asian features, sleek dark hair tied back neatly, was by his side. Her accent, like his own, was upstate NYC. She had smiled, revealing even, white teeth. 'Not that you are old!'

Hajime had smiled too. 'I am more intrigued by their skill with phone cameras than by their beauty.'

'Oh, but beauty is the real thing. The other is just a gross motor skill. It can be acquired with practise. It's like hammering metal sheets. You do it a sufficient number of times and you perfect the strokes.' She had glanced at the group still occupying the bridge. 'Do you think the dues of politeness have been paid and I can wade through? I really need to get to the other side.'

After a long time Hajime had felt light-hearted. 'You sound like you are from my neighbourhood in New York, let me help. I will soon have you safe and dry on the other shore.'

They had crossed the bridge together, in step. Pausing amidst the moving crowd on the other side, Haruko had held out her hand. 'Thank you. Given that there are only two possible directions on a bridge and you were facing this way, I am assuming I did not bring you out of your way.'

'I hate to disagree so early in our acquaintance, but you are wrong. There are, in fact, three possible and one impossible direction on any bridge.'

'Really?'

'Of course, the third possible one being over the side.'

'And the impossible?'

'Up in the air! But you couldn't have brought me out of my way even if you had tried. Fact is, I am still looking for my way. And a cup of coffee.'

'One quest at least ends right now. I see a Starbucks.'

Over coffee, Haruko had told him about her own quest. She had trained in jewellery craft and gem cutting, and was looking for a shop-cum-studio to rent. 'Everyone told me that Singapore is a glorified shopping mall, and yet it is more difficult to find a place here than it was in Bombay.'

Meena had floated past Hajime again. 'You have lived in India much?'

'Over two years. Jaipur, Bombay, Cuttack, Benares. I still visit from time to time. I have a partner working with me there, an awesome goldsmith. I also get my stones cut and polished there, but I set them myself. With my own hands.' Haruko had spread her long fingers. 'It's not an easy place, India. It does not let you hold it at arm's length. You either like it very much or can't stand it.'

'And you liked it very much at first, and then couldn't stand it?'

'Not quite.' Haruko had smiled carefully. 'I learnt a chunk of what I needed to learn there. But Sing is by far the best for business. Besides, I like it here. The insipidness gives me space to work and visualize, to escape a bit.'

Hajime had looked out at the bustling waterfront. Meena might be in a café too, trying to escape a bit. *We killed Yuri*, she had said, but she was wrong. It was Yuri who, in the insidious way of the weak, had killed them.

'If insipidity is what you seek,' he had said, 'it is aplenty here.'

'That is harsh!'

'I teach graduate class in modern literature at the NUS. Harshness is part of the curriculum.'

Haruko had laughed and then whipped out her phone. 'Oh, do you see that beetle there? What a gorgeous colour!' She had trained the phone camera's single eye on the brown-gold bug crawling across the polished table and had clicked several pictures. 'A perfect model for a brooch or hair ornament, a small cat's-eye beetle on a gold leaf!' She had pulled out a small notebook from her tote bag and torn a page. 'Here's my number. What's yours? I must continue with my search now, I have a viewing arranged for this evening. But,' she had paused and smiled, 'I have a good feeling about our meeting.'

Hajime had written his number at the back of her notebook, and they had parted.

That night, as on numerous others, he had reread the only email Meena had written to him after leaving Tokyo: *We killed Yuri, you and I, and it changed everything. Death changed life.* He had looked up flights to Delhi again. There were thirty-two flights in all, thirty-two ways of not reaching Meena. His sleep had been broken by dreams, and classes the next day had seemed like a chore. During the course of the week, he had lost the paper with Haruko's number.

HE HAD FAILED to recognize Haruko's voice when she had called a few weeks later.

'I had called earlier, but there was no answer.'

There had been missed calls on his mobile phone but he hadn't recognized the number, hadn't called back.

'So sorry. I teach classes in the morning and again late in the afternoon, so I might have missed your call.'

'That's all right, I don't give up easy! You remember I said

I had a good feeling? I was so right, you were very lucky for me. After meeting you that day, I found the perfect place at Boat Quay – the right size, good light, lots of footfall, but exclusive. I have already moved in. And do you remember the beetle? I have made a first model from it. Have dinner with me tomorrow and I will show you.'

He had switched the phone from one ear to the other. He was unable to picture her. Only the merest impression of her and their meeting had remained, a vague memory of an athletic woman with typical, brace-straightened American teeth.

'Let me see. Dinner during the week is always a bit difficult.'

'Tomorrow night is the only night I have. I must work on the model again from the day after and complete the final pieces in the next three weeks. Come on.' Her voice was rich with laughter. 'You might enjoy spending time with me!'

He had met Haruko the next night at a fashionable steakhouse at Boat Quay. He was surprised at how striking she looked. She wore a white shirt dress which left her long, toned legs bare, lime-green espadrilles, and a collar-like necklace with distinctive lime-green enamel work. She had kissed Hajime warmly on both cheeks like an old friend, and led him to a corner table.

'Do you like the restaurant?' she had asked. 'I picked it because it is the closest to my studio. Let's get the food out of the way. You order. I eat everything.'

He had scrutinized the menu carefully and ordered their dinner – Kobe beef, creamed spinach, some crab cakes. Haruko had eaten undiscriminatingly, spooning the spinach over the crab cakes, ruining their crisp crusts, almost mincing the marbled, delicate beef. During the meal, she had spoken about jewellery craft, assuming his interest in it in a way that he had found charming. Her single-minded focus on her work filled Hajime with amazement.

'Jewellery making is a craft, an art and a precise science all rolled into one,' she had said. 'There's many parts to it – metalwork, and assessing the quality of crystals and stones, and stone setting and enamelling which are just craftwork and chemistry, but there are other aspects like aesthetics and designing and proportion which are pure art.'

'It is obviously not just a profession for you.'

'It is my life's work,' she had said simply.

After dinner, they had walked to her studio. It was a large, street-facing unit, with the front room fitted out like a living room. There were large photographs of Haruko on the walls – working at a draughtsman's desk, polishing, crafting. The carpet-less floor was of a highly polished beige-coloured stone, and there were sofas strewn around, covered in many-hued silks. Haruko's work was on display in glass cases scattered around the room. Even to Hajime, who knew nothing about jewellery, the ornaments were beautiful. Only later did he learn that she was famous, her work well known and commanding a devoted following.

'I am old school. I like my pieces to have form. They are all smooth and well-proportioned and heavy. Quite a few of them are solid. I cast everything by hand, make my own moulds. Come this way.'

She had led him through a door into a room furnished like a workshop. There was a draughtsman's table, with papers and a lamp in one corner. A long workbench ran down the middle of the room, fitted with a small, portable furnace on one end. Small, fine-looking implements, beakers of liquids, boxes with gleaming bits of metals and stones, were arranged neatly along its length. A futon with pillows and cushions was set against the wall furthest from the door.

Haruko had flung her arm out. 'This is where I live, how I live.' She had picked up an ornament placed on a square piece of blue chamois leather from the workbench and held it out to Hajime. 'Here, this is the one inspired by the beetle we met the other day.' The ornament was shaped like a gold frond, each minute leaf distinct on its delicate stalk. It was studded with golden-brown beetles, their tiny gold legs gripping leaf and stalk. 'The beetles are detachable. You can remove them and place them on a different leaf.'

Hajime was astonished, dazed by the fragile fineness of the ornament. 'It is stunning – a work of art.' He had looked at her in wonder. 'You are an artist.'

Haruko had laughed delightedly. 'And it surprises you? That is funny!'

Replacing the ornament carefully on the blue leather square, he had taken Haruko's hands in his own and examined her long, strong fingers, her unpainted nails, her veins running blue at the base of her wrist.

She had looked on and then, leaning towards him, had kissed him on the mouth. 'I have been meaning to do this for a while.' She had disengaged one of her hands and held it to his face, framing his cheek and jaw. Hajime had drawn her closer, pressing her to him, and she had kissed him again, this time parting his lips, sliding her tongue into his mouth. Then she had drawn back. 'Sorry, can't do anything more tonight. I have to sleep at eleven sharp. I begin work at five a.m. tomorrow. I need to make ten of these, each by hand, and I have a schedule I must keep to.'

The blood rushing in Hajime's ears had made it difficult for him to understand what she said. Dazed, he had reached for her.

'Really, I have these rules. And I never break them.' Haruko's eyes were like lit windows. She grazed his cheek with her fingers. 'But perhaps I can do something for you.' She had knelt before him and had undone the buttons of his trousers, touching him with her strong, slightly rough fingers. She had bent her head, her mouth sliding over him, her tongue probing him. Hajime had tried to draw her closer, but she had shaken his hand off, placing her own on his buttocks instead, pulling him towards her, moving all over him at her will. Her mouth was soft, wet, and Hajime had exploded with sensations, his nerves touched to the quick. The release had flooded his body and Haruko had fallen back on her haunches, wiping her mouth, the front of her dress stained.

She had looked up at him, amused. 'Did that do you good? Next time, try to remember my name. It is hardly the thing to call out someone else's name at such a time!' She was laughing as she rose to her feet and looked at her watch. 'Ten forty-five. I have fifteen minutes to brush my teeth, take off these clothes and be in bed. Bye for now. Sorry to rush, but I can't not be in bed by eleven. I will call once my pieces are done.'

Hajime was out of the door in minutes, still confused. He had walked for some distance before hailing a cab, but the sultry humid air had done nothing to clear his thoughts.

AFTER THAT NIGHT, Hajime had not heard from Haruko for several weeks. His calls went unanswered. Then, one evening, she had called. As if she was continuing an interrupted conversation, she had said, 'You remember the Starbucks near the Helix Bridge? I am there now. And would you believe it, the twin of that golden bug is here too! Come, I will show you pictures of my final pieces. They are all sold.'

They soon settled into a pattern. Hajime learnt about the self-made rituals Haruko followed while working – always wearing the same tattered old apron, the implements on the workbench arranged in a certain order, the air conditioning always at 23.5 degrees. She would wake up at four thirty in the morning, have three cups of black coffee and toast for breakfast, and be at her workbench at five sharp. In the middle of the day, she would take a break to do a high-intensity exercise routine for thirty minutes, eat her lunch and go right back to work. She would work until late in the evening, in utter silence, not speaking unless absolutely essential. While she worked, everything else ceased to exist for her. Hajime reverted to the life he had lived before he met her during her work phases. He went for a run in the Botanical Gardens, taught classes, volunteered at the local dog shelter, read in the evenings. When she was between projects and inspiration, she called, always suddenly, always picking the thread up from where they had left. They went out for dinner and returned to Haruko's studio to make love on the futon in her work room.

Once, Hajime offered to cook a meal for her. Though his kitchen was well equipped, with a high-end cooking range, expensive pots and pans, he usually cooked quick, functional meals of boiled rice and fish for himself. For Haruko, he planned an elaborate dinner and shopped carefully for the ingredients for pasta and salad and tiramisu on his way back from the university. He sat a large pan filled with water to boil and began shredding salad leaves. But his arms felt heavy, each action seemed difficult, he was overcome with fatigue. The thought of cooking – chopping and boiling and crumbling and mixing – exhausted him. He binned the salad leaves, turned off the induction cooker and called Haruko. She was okay with the change of plans and he took her to an Italian restaurant in Holland Village instead.

Over dinner, Hajime told her about his life in Kyoto for the first time. About Meena, and Yuri. Haruko looked at him intently as he told her how he had raced to Meena's apartment to find the paramedics already there, Yuri's white, brittle-looking body on a stretcher, covered with Meena's colourful quilt, blood drying in the bathtub.

'There was a post-mortem, a police inquiry ... They concluded it was suicide. Yuri's aunt from Kobe came down for the funeral. She wouldn't let Meena or me have anything to do with it. In the end, we just sent wreaths.' Hajime paused, realizing that he had ground his spaghetti into a mess with his fork. 'She didn't cry during all that time. It was only when everything was over that she cried, soundlessly, night after night, lying flat on her back, her pillow damp with tears every morning. I stayed over, cooked meals, tried to talk to her about things that had interested us. But I couldn't reach her ... I didn't realize then, but she had gone too, perhaps when Yuri had ... And all the while, as I was trying very hard to be with her, she was quietly preparing to leave. One night, she just came out and told me, *I am going back tomorrow.* Just like that...'

Hajime found it difficult to continue. Haruko shook her head. 'How unnecessarily messy and unpleasant.' They ate in silence for some time.

'What I could never understand is why she would leave like that,' Hajime spoke again. 'Without giving us a real chance, without trying to figure out what had happened to us, together. She just decided on her own and left. In utter silence.'

'It is difficult enough to understand our own actions. It is never of any use to analyse someone else's actions or motives, Hajime. It happened.' Haruko sipped her wine. 'Kyoto is lovely, it must have been something to see all the seasons there. I have been there once, in fall. The trees were on fire and all the paths were copper red. I did a collection with fall leaves as the motif,' she said. 'I have an idea ... Let's go to Kyoto to see the cherries bloom.'

Hajime set down his garlic bread – it was dry and crusty – and drank some water. 'No,' he said. 'No, I don't want to see the cherry blossoms in Kyoto.'

Haruko looked at him, holding his gaze with her own. 'Perhaps you are right, cherry blossoms are a bit passé. And anyway, their season's passed for this year. But let's take a holiday. I must have one now.'

'Why now?'

'Because it is June and we have known each other for almost a year, and my head seems to be filled with

Singapore's concrete blocks and plastic flowers. Are those sufficient reasons?'

It was more than a year since the night he had last seen Meena. 'Sure, those are enough reasons. A holiday would be good. I'll do some research. Which part of the world would you like to see?'

'A part I have seen. We will go to Borneo, to the Turtle Island in the Sulu Sea. They call it Pulau Selingan. You will like it. It never fails to rekindle my jaded imagination. It is simply amazing, white and blue and blissful. Do you know that turtles travel from all over the world to lay eggs there, right where they themselves began life as hatchlings?'

The next day, Hajime went to Kinokuniya and bought the Lonely Planet guide to Borneo. He read about its rainforests and its scintillating wildlife, the orangutans and proboscis monkeys and myriad birds. Compared to the brilliant jungles, the Turtle Island seemed rather tame.

Haruko shook her head when he suggested a resort on the Kinabatangan river, deep in the rainforests. 'No, no. Jungles are crowded places. You'll see. Though the log chalets and facilities are very basic, the Turtle Island is fascinating.'

HAJIME INSPECTED THE dishes set out on the long tables in the lunch hall. They had breakfasted early in the tiny port town of Sandakan before catching the speedboat to Selingan and were ravenous by lunchtime. The food was disappointing. There was boiled cabbage, tofu and bamboo shoots in a nondescript brown sauce, stringy morning glory, overcooked rice.

Haruko filled the plastic compartments in her tray with the food and talked about the turtles as she ate. 'It is astounding, the effort the mother turtle makes. Swimming from the other end of the earth to lay these eggs. Imagine the conviction, the commitment that nature compels.'

Hajime poked the wet cabbage leaves with a plastic fork. 'To lay slimy little eggs which may or may not hatch, into hatchlings which may or may not live and, if they do, will have to repeat the whole tedious, exhausting cycle again and again?'

'Yes, absolutely. This is her life's work. Whether it amounts to anything, whether it succeeds or fails, that's of no relevance.'

After lunch, they walked back to their chalet.

'I must sleep for an hour. I have to begin working on the drawings tomorrow, and tonight we shall be up late to watch the turtle. You might like to rest as well.'

Haruko slipped out of her clothes and was soon breathing evenly, her long, naked body loose in repose. Hajime lay beside her on the spartan bed and tried to sleep, but the daylight was too bright behind his closed eyes. After a quarter of an hour, he gave up and rose. He was hungry and rummaged in his bag for something to eat. There was a packet of biscuits, a couple of apples. The packet rustled as he tried to tear it open, and Haruko turned in her sleep. Hajime carefully put the biscuits and apples in his pockets and quietly opened the old wardrobe in the corner. He took out a cotton quilt, covered Haruko's naked body, and stepped out, pulling the door of the chalet shut behind him.

The beach was a white blaze. The tide had receded, leaving glimmering shells and odd-looking pieces of coral strewn along the waterline. Hajime bent down to examine the tiny white and red molluscs wriggling in the sand when he caught a movement from the corner of his eye.

Turning, he saw the great monitor from earlier in the day. It was still nestled among the broad green leaves. As Hajime watched, it stirred and tilted its glossy head to one side. Hajime could see its eye, like a large bead, revolve and focus on him.

He pulled out an apple and rolled it towards the lizard. 'Won't your majesty eat this apple?' he muttered.

The lizard swivelled its head downwards and looked at the fruit, bright red on the white sand. A gull swooped low overhead, and the monitor stuck a claw out with startling quickness. It grabbed the apple and settled back deep among the leaves. Hajime lay down in the sand, hands under his head, and watched the lizard eat the entire apple – skin, flesh and core – its head held regally aloft. Then it sat on its haunches and regarded Hajime.

Hajime shook his head. 'I have nothing more, except for the confusion that fills me and which I would happily give to you to devour. But you need to eat me to get to it. And I am pretty bitter at the moment, you will not enjoy me.' The monitor remained motionless, except for a brief movement of its tail hidden among the leaves, causing them to rustle. 'I don't enjoy me at present either. My students don't enjoy my lectures, I am certain the girl at Circle K does not enjoy bagging my purchases, I suspect you do not enjoy the sight of me. The only person who seems to enjoy me is Haruko.' The lizard lowered its head. 'You agree. A king can afford to be honest, he has no need to lie or conceal. A king can speak his mind. Or not – just as he chooses. I am of course not a king, and Haruko does not care enough to be one. You are ancient and a king from the beginning of time. Perhaps you understand why the turtle comes here to lay slimy eggs and why have we come to watch her do so. Pointless eggs. Pointless people.'

The sun was declining redly. Despite the bloodbath in the west, the sea was still innocently blue. He heard Haruko's voice calling him and sat up, dusting sand off himself.

'What a sunset!' Haruko came up to him, smiling. 'There's a stone quarried in Sri Lanka called the padparadscha – the western sky is exactly that colour. Gorgeous!' She looked at him. 'What have you been doing with yourself? There is sand in your hair.'

'I was talking to the monitor. It is a good conversationalist.'

'It is a lazy lizard, lolling all day on the beach. Come, let's have some tea and toast. I am hungry.'

She turned and walked inland. Hajime followed, bowing silently to the motionless monitor.

THE SHORT TROPICAL dusk was soon over and night fell swiftly. The electric lights on the island were few and feeble. Travelling turtles landed under the cover of darkness and the beach was forbidden to visitors at night.

Hajime paced the open courtyard outside the dining hall where turtle-watchers had congregated. His pockets bulged with the fruits he had taken from the fruit dish at dinner. He cast a look at Haruko sitting cross-legged on the low wall of the courtyard, eyes closed, doing her breathing exercises, and quietly stepped out into the night.

The path to the beach was dark, and shadows slipped and glided all around. The beach glimmered sliver. He could see the torch beams of the patrolling Sea Rangers further down, and the shimmering phosphorescence in the sea. He walked along until he reached the clump of weeds. A darker shadow rose from the shadowy patch.

'I knew you would be waiting for me,' Hajime whispered as he pulled the fruits out of his pockets. 'I apologize for the monotonous diet, but the cooked food is not worth touching. Hope you enjoy this. Bon appétit.'

The monitor turned until it was silhouetted against the beach, its neck bent in Hajime's direction. The ranger's whistle sounded shrilly.

'Good night. I shall be back in the morning.'

Hajime walked back towards the dining hall. The sky was like an inverted rice bowl, the stars spilt in sticky clusters. The shrubs were dotted with green-glowing fireflies. Hajime carefully caught one in his cupped palms. When he reached the courtyard, the Rangers were rounding up the turtle watchers.

'Just in time!' Haruko said. 'I was going to leave. We must hurry, the turtle is ready.'

'See.' Hajime held his joined palms before Haruko. The light of the firefly glimmered thought the cracks between his fingers. 'It has been lighting the night.' He opened his hands slowly and the firefly escaped from its temporary prison.

'What is it? Oh, a glow worm. They are everywhere.' She turned towards the beach. 'Let's go now.'

They followed the Rangers on to the beach. In the yellow beams of their powerful torches, a bulky shape was revealed. It was a hornbill turtle, its carapace as big as a large umbrella, squatting over a hole in the sand. Hajime looked at the turtle's glazed eyes and mournful mouth. It seemed to him that the turtle was in pain.

'The mother is tired, very tired,' the Ranger conducting the show explained. 'Imagine competing in a freestyle swimming meet, followed by a cross-country run, and ending with an endurance trial. That's what the mother has done during the course of the past weeks and months, multiplied many times over. Tonight, she has dug a hole and is finally ready to release the eggs.'

As if on cue, several shiny eggs, the size of tennis balls, fell into the pit in the sand. Dark liquid oozed from the turtle's eyes.

'Poor beast. Poor, poor beast,' Hajime muttered.

Haruko turned her head and looked at him with a smile. 'The mother is in a trance. She is fulfilling her purpose. She is creating. This is her life's work.'

After the turtle finished laying its eggs, it wearily shuffled off the pit and began covering it with sand, the flippers moving slowly, so slowly that each complete movement seemed to take several minutes. When it finished, it began shuffling down the beach, back to the sea. The Rangers quickly reopened the nest the tired turtle had built with infinite effort and scooped up the eggs into buckets.

'The eggs have a better chance of hatching under our protection,' the Ranger explained as his colleagues carried the buckets away to the hatcheries.

It was past eleven o'clock when they got back to their chalet. Haruko needed to work on her design the next morning. She hugged Hajime quickly, briefly rubbing her palms up and down his back. 'I am rather like that turtle. There are only two things I really, really care about – doing my life's work and having sex with you. Sex will have to wait though.' She kissed him with her smiling mouth and undressed with her usual speed. She was in bed and fast asleep by the time Hajime had showered and changed into his pyjamas.

Hajime lay awake listening to the roar of the sea, and thought about the monitor on the beach. He imagined it prowling around in the territory it ruled, hunting the salamanders, moles, shrews and other creatures of the night as the fancy took him.

THE ROOM WAS flooded with sunlight when Hajime woke up. Turning, he checked the time on his phone. Ten a.m. He slowly sat up. The bed was hard, and he felt stiff all over. There was a plastic tray on the table by his bedside, with a few bread rolls and muffins, some fruit, plastic cutlery. A slip of paper dangled from under a bunch of bananas. *Got you breakfast,* the unsigned note read. *You were so beautifully asleep! Am working on my drawings. See you in the evening.*

Through the door, he could see Haruko on the veranda, her back to the room, sitting cross-legged, bent over the small folding desk she had brought along. Her leather case containing drawing pencils, and her folios and papers lay beside her. He quickly showered, tucked his e-reader under his arm, and walked out with the breakfast tray. Haruko did not look up as he passed by.

The beach was less incandescent than yesterday. There were stray clouds in the sky and the fine sand was cool in the moving patches of shade. The monitor had emerged from its clump of weeds. It had a massive, broad body, with folds of skin, rust, black and grey in colour, hanging from its sides. Its powerful dark tail lay curved like a bold question mark on the sand.

Hajime lowered the plastic tray on to the sand and sat a short distance from it, his legs folded awkwardly. Picking up a couple of muffins, he rolled them gently towards the monitor. It caught the food with its forepaws, its near eye fixed on Hajime.

'I hope the breakfast is to your taste,' Hajime said. 'Haruko had hers before I woke up. Even if I were awake, she would have eaten alone, wouldn't have said a word to me. It is a rule with her when she works.' Hajime buttered a bread roll and began eating. 'She has many rules. She sleeps naked, never eats grapefruit, must have two glasses of water with every meal. She is very strong, terrific at sex, can send me through the roof if she wishes, *when* she wishes. She seems to have little past and no interest in the future. She is right here, right now. I don't know much about her, besides her work. She told me once that she was born in Hong Kong, in springtime. Her Japanese mother named her Haruko, which means the child of spring. And, of course, in the kanji script, "ha" could stand for Hong Kong too. Poetic and clever, isn't it? And what does she think about it?' Hajime paused and stuck his plastic knife in the sand. 'Nothing, absolutely nothing. It is a mere bunch of words. It brings no images which she could translate into metal or stone or wood or clay.' He pushed the plastic tray aside and stretched his legs. 'I still dream of Meena some nights. I see her plainly – fresh after a bath, her wet hair down her back, a towel wrapped around her moist body. In my dream, I have made breakfast – eggs and toast and grapefruit juice and coffee. I pull her on to my lap, her towel feels damp on my thighs. *I can feel you*, she whispers, turning red. Then I wake up. If I fall asleep again, there she is once more, standing in the doorway, her satchel slung across her body, a bag of oranges swinging from her hand...' Hajime broke off and rolled some of the fruit towards the lizard. 'I never dream of Meena as I saw her last. I don't need to. I can see her still, sitting at the table in the tiny living room, laptop open, her back to the kitchenette where I am washing kabu. There is soba cooking in the pot, I have broken open a fresh packet that evening. I have crumbled seaweed and minced tofu ready for seasoning it. She speaks over her shoulder to me. *I have surrendered my fellowship at Kyodai*, she says. *I'll leave for Tokyo tomorrow*. I see her in profile, her eyes still on the screen of the laptop as she tells me that she has accepted a job in Delhi, that she will leave Japan for good soon, as soon as she can. I quietly turn the burner off, pick up my overnight bag and leave. I don't say a word, not a single word. I can't.' He bit into an apple and rose. 'I don't want to wear you out all at once. I will go and try to find some coffee. And perhaps swim afterwards.'

The breakfast was long over and the dining hall was empty, but a friendly Bornean girl got him a cup of coffee from the staff kitchen. She spoke little English, and blushed when Hajime pointed to her and made a little heart with his index fingers and thumbs. Afterwards, he lay about on the beach, reading or gazing out at the sea. He swam a little in the shallows. The current was strong, and he stayed close to the shore. He caught a glimpse of Haruko at lunch as she left the dining hall, food tray in hand, eyes fixed on the ground. The Bornean girl from the morning was near the buffet tables. He pointed at the food and then at his stomach and shaking his head pretended to keel over. The girl laughed and disappeared inside the kitchen. She returned with a thick ceramic platter filled with breakfast breads, a large pat of butter and some fruit. Hajime retreated to the beach with his meal. The monitor appeared to be asleep, and he left a portion of his food near the clump. He ate looking out at the sea which was a deeper blue under the cloudy sky. High waves washed on the beach above the watermark. Then, switching on his e-reader, he lay in the sand rereading the *Dream of the Red Chamber*.

He must have dozed off, for he was awakened by Haruko's exclamations. She was taking pictures of the changing colours of sunset.

'Oh God!' She turned to him. 'Isn't it unfair that these colours fade away before I can memorize them? The photos never capture them accurately.'

He sat up, rubbing his eyes. Laughing, she hung the camera on his shoulder and, taking his hand, led him to the end of the beach, away from the chalets. There, behind a large rock, she took off her tunic. The setting sun threw red highlights on her firm body as she knelt before him. Through his paroxysm of pleasure, Hajime saw Haruko looking at him, her mouth curved in a smile.

THAT EVENING, THEY strolled towards the dinner hall hand in hand, and Haruko talked about the difficulties in her drawings.

'I need to redo the first few. The lines are not quite right, but I have enough material for at least half a dozen models.' She stepped around a monitor which lay right across the path. 'By the way, did you see the big guy on the beach again today?'

'Sure. I spent the day with him, same as yesterday. He's good company and doesn't mind the monotonous food.'

Haruko frowned. 'You should not give it food. You never know, it might be harmful for it. It is a predator, not a domestic animal.'

They walked on in silence. As they neared the turtle-watchers' courtyard, Hajime spoke. 'I don't want to watch the turtle tonight. It seems very intrusive, surrounding her and staring, when she has come all this distance to be private.'

'Sure, but come and see the hatchlings going home to the sea.'

The dinner was colourless soup, watery curry, wilted bok choy and fruits. Hajime ate some bread rolls with his soup and filled his pockets with apples and longans.

Haruko looked up as she ladled the curry over a helping of mushy rice. 'For the big guy? You really shouldn't, Hajime. It did not grow so big without being able to look after itself. You are not helping. We are all self-sustaining and, most of the time, if we are left alone and not meddled with, we do just fine.'

Hajime chewed the hard bread roll then, setting his tray down on the table, softly touched Haruko's ear, tracing the line of her delicate jaw. 'Come to the beach, Haruko. The sky has upended itself, there are stars spilt everywhere.'

Haruko got up. She had finished eating. 'That would be breaking all rules!'

'Yes,' Hajime agreed. 'Come anyway.'

Haruko smiled, stacked their trays one over the other, and kissed him on the cheek. She then walked out of the dinner hall and sat cross-legged on the courtyard wall, eyes closed, and began her breathing exercise.

Hajime strolled to the beach. Clouds were building in towering heaps in the west, and the patch of weeds was deserted. Hajime stood, irresolute, until he caught a movement under a bit of rock close by. The monitor emerged from behind the rock and stood bobbing its head. Hajime placed the food on the sand.

'Good evening. I see you were waiting for me,' he said. 'Haruko says I ought not to feed you. She does not see that I am not feeding you at all. I am nourishing myself. I am starved, and you are sustaining me.'

The monitor approached with its shuffling gait, its great tail dragging behind it, dark against the white sand. Hajime squatted at some distance and watched it devour the food. From time to time, it raised the soft-sloped triangle of its head and tilted it towards Hajime. When the first drops of rain fell, it grabbed what remained of the fruits in its mouth and shuffled back behind the rocks. Hajime got up. There was a large shallow depression in the sand where the monitor had been.

Haruko met him on the path leading to the turtle-watchers' courtyard. 'I came to find you. You must not miss the hatchlings.'

She took Hajime's hand and they walked to the other end of the beach. The Rangers were already emptying buckets filled with little turtles on to the wet sand. The tiny creatures were scuttling over each other, slipping, sliding, tumbling in their haste to enter the sea. 'We release them at night,' the Ranger from the previous night explained. 'It helps them avoid the gulls and the sea eagles. The dark provides them cover, but their travails are not over – there are crabs and other predators waiting in the shallow waters. And in the deep sea, still other dangers. They'll need to be very clever and very, very lucky to survive.'

Hajime stood looking at their headlong flight, his hand still in Haruko's. 'So after all this fumbling in the dark, all these precautions, there is no safety for them, even in their own element...'

Haruko shrugged.

THE NEXT MORNING was clear. The wind at night had swept away all clouds. This was their last day on the island. They had to begin their journey back the next morning.

Hajime swam and read and took walks on the beach. The monitor rested on the moist sand and turned its beady eyes towards him from time to time. At lunch, Hajime could not find the Bornean girl from the day before and filled his plastic tray with steamed rice, sautéed snow peas, last night's wilted bok choy and some gingery tofu. He was famished and ate the food. He took a second helping and carried it to the beach. The monitor examined the unfamiliar food with one eye as Hajime set it down.

'This was the best I could do. Try the tofu, it is not entirely inedible. And if all else fails, there is always rice. It fills you up, sticks to your insides like secrets. Try it, who knows you might like it. And when you have eaten your fill, you could consider answering my questions. About the turtles. And the hatchlings. Meena, Haruko and I. The sea and the sky. And why can't I fly?' He rose. 'I know, I am a puerile poet. No particular talent for anything. Except when I was with Meena. Then I had something ... Can't quite say what. The words rained unrestrained then, free from rules. No longer though.' The monitor had begun eating. 'I see you eat with a dignified eagerness, it's not entirely unpalatable to you. I will leave you to it. I must make the most of my last day here. Why must I? That is another question I don't know the answer to.'

Hajime walked through the island, past the egg enclosures and down the path Haruko and he had taken the first day. He saw the blue salamanders again, the ones Haruko had admired, playing in the sand. A whole nest of them, flickering and gleaming.

He had an idea and returned to the chalet. Haruko was hard at work after lunch. He entered quietly and extracted a large transparent bottle filled with vitamin pills from his bag. Emptying the pills into a Ziploc bag, he punched some holes into the lid of the bottle with a ballpoint pen, and carried it along with a hand towel from the bathroom back to where the salamanders ran.

He targeted one, small and vividly blue, and stalked it patiently. At last, the salamander sat still on a pebble. He trapped it in the towel and shook it gently into the empty bottle, quickly screwing the lid in place. The salamander lashed around in the small bottle, scrambling and falling, mad with fear. Eventually, when it stopped struggling, he caught a few beetles and insects and slipped them into the bottle.

The sun was declining and Hajime retraced his steps towards the beach.

Haruko was already there. 'The first drafts are almost finished,' she said, stretching her arms. 'This has been a fantastic break.'

Hajime held up the plastic bottle. 'I caught this for you. It took some doing. I have been feeding it live bugs to keep it interested.'

Haruko looked at the salamander as it lay motionless at the bottom of the bottle and raised her eyes to him. 'But I have memorized this colour already. I don't need to see it again.'

She took the jar from Hajime's hands and, unscrewing the lid, tilted it towards the sand. The salamander uncoiled itself and slipped out swiftly. It ran across the beach, the colour in its tail flickering like a tiny beacon on the white sand.

From nowhere, the monitor appeared. With breath-taking suddenness, and a movement precise and economical like a Sumo wrestler's, it caught the speeding salamander in its mouth.

Haruko shrieked and screwed her eyes shut. Hajime stood motionless.

Finally, he heard the monitor answer his questions as it swallowed the salamander: *The turtle's stupid. All shores are the same. You are the sea. Roll endlessly.*

ACKNOWLEDGEMENTS

There are places because of which *Kintsugi* got written – the onsen in Hakone, the bamboo forest of Arashiyama, the turtle islands in Borneo, the bylanes and bazaars of Jaipur. And people without whom *Kintsugi* wouldn't have existed – friends Som, Siddhartha Gigoo and Madhu Jain who encouraged me in my stumbling efforts; Shinie Antony who gave timely and excellent feedback; my editor, Rahul Soni without whose careful and kind nurture *Kintsugi* wouldn't have taken its present form, Sohini Basak whose close reading and insightful observations helped shape the book, and my publisher, Udayan Mitra whose belief in my work held me up through bouts of severe self-doubt; my father Dr Surendra Upadhyay, who gave me all my words, and my mother Puja Upadhyay, who gave all of herself; my father-in-law and mother-in-law, Krishan Kumar Sharma and Girija Sharma, my sister, sisters-in-law, brothers-in-law, nieces, nephews and cousins, who created an affectionate and nurturing environment; my husband, Vikas Sharma, who introduced me to Japan and her beauty, and my son Yashodhar who accompanied me in all my rambles, they heroically listened to parts of this unfinished work when I could no longer bear to look at it on my own. Towards all of them, my gratitude is unbounded, inexpressible, eternal.

30 Years *of*

HarperCollins *Publishers* India

At HarperCollins, we believe in telling the best stories and finding the widest possible readership for our books in every format possible. We started publishing 30 years ago; a great deal has changed since then, but what has remained constant is the passion with which our authors write their books, the love with which readers receive them, and the sheer joy and excitement that we as publishers feel in being a part of the publishing process.

Over the years, we've had the pleasure of publishing some of the finest writing from the subcontinent and around the world, and some of the biggest bestsellers in India's publishing history. Our books and authors have won a phenomenal range of awards, and we ourselves have been named Publisher of the Year the greatest number of times. But nothing has meant more to us than the fact that millions of people have read the books we published, and somewhere, a book of ours might have made a difference.

As we step into our fourth decade, we go back to that one word – a word which has been a driving force for us all these years.

Read.